Octavia Bloom

and the

Missing Key

ESTELLE GRACE TUDOR

★ ★ ★ ★ ★ ★ ★

Inlustris

First published in the UK in 2020 by Inlustris Publishing, Wales
Text © Estelle Grace Tudor, 2020
Cover designed by 100 Covers © Map by Adam Charters ©
'Wattle' Artwork by Adam Tudor ©
Interior formatting and design by Evenstar Books ©
Inlustris Publishing, 2020

A CIP catalogue record for this book is available from the British Library.

Paperback ISBN 978 1 8380292 0 3

E-book ISBN 978 1 8380292 1 0

Hardback ISBN 978 1 8380292 2 7

Printed in the UK

For my magic ones...
Dean, Adam, Chloe,
Nathan & Jake.

Contents

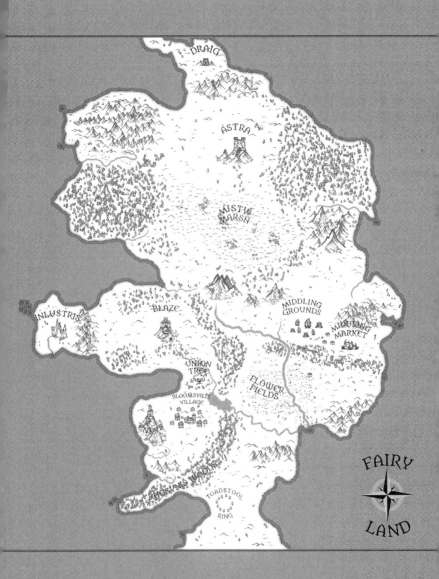

DRAIG

ÁSTRA

MISTY
MARSH

INDUSTRIS

BLAZE

MIDDLING
GROUNDS

MIDDLING
MARKET

UNION
TREE

FLOWER
FIELDS

BLOOMSVILLE
VILLAGE

RHOSYN'S WOODS

TOADSTOOL
RING

FAIRY
LAND

One

Hide-and-Seek

CROUCHED DOWN, QUIET AS A MOUSE, Octavia Bloom was holding her breath.

The dust floating like glitter in the old attic was tickling her nose. Laughter bubbled up inside her, which she quickly suppressed by biting down on her lip. It wouldn't do to make a noise and give away her position as she hid behind the old striped sofa. If she kept quiet, she was certain to win this round of hide-and-seek. Her sister and cousins wouldn't think to look up here. The attic at Grandmother's house was strictly forbidden.

Well, it was a castle, rather than a house, cut into the craggy cliffs of the Cornish coast. Checking that she was still alone, Octavia crept over to the arched window and looked down at the thundering waves below. As she stared

at the swirling water, she imagined great battles being fought and terrifying pirates having many adventures here. Octavia wasn't afraid, though; she was nearly ten, thank you very much. This wasn't the first time she had sneaked up to the attic, looking for adventures of her own. At this very moment her pocket was stuffed with handfuls of moss and her little doll. The patch of weak sunlight underneath the window was perfect for playing fairyland in.

Nibbling absentmindedly on a biscuit she had snatched from the kitchen, she thought about which part of the castle to explore next time. There was certainly much to discover in this draughty old castle – secret nooks and winding tunnels, perfect for a game of hide-and-seek. The last time Octavia had been hiding in Grandmother's bedroom, she had fallen against a brick sticking out of the wall near the window. It had pushed into the wall, revealing a secret drawer in the window seat. In it was her grandmother's charm bracelet and some pieces of crinkled parchment. Octavia wiped the crumbs from her mouth as she remembered the drawings of exotic-looking flowers she had seen on the top sheet. That wasn't really surprising; her grandmother was a keen gardener and spent many hours with her hands wrist-deep in soil in the Castle hot-house.

Deep in thought, Octavia jumped as a hand clamped down onto her shoulder.

"Found you!" a gleeful voice sing-songed. Octavia

looked up to see her older sister, Felicity.

"How did you find me?" she asked, disappointed that her little hideaway had been found.

Felicity frowned, shaking the dust from her cotton skirt. "You left the door ajar, silly! Now come on – you know we're not allowed up here. We promised Grandmother, and we don't want her to tell Mum and Dad that we're not sticking to her rules."

Octavia pulled a face. "I don't see why we have to follow the rules at all. If Mum and Dad didn't go off every school holiday, they could be here having fun with us."

Felicity looked at Octavia and sighed, before explaining for what Octavia felt was the hundredth time. "You know they go on important research trips with Aunt and Uncle. They have their company to run and natural medicines to make that help people, Tavi," she admonished, hands on her hips.

"I know that," Octavia said with exasperation, "but I wish just once they'd take us with them. I'd love to explore a steamy rainforest or visit the far east." Her expression grew dreamy as she imagined the adventures she would have.

Felicity threw up her hands, and a smile twitched at the corner of her lips. "Come on. It's nearly teatime, and Martha and Beatrice have already gone down."

At the mention of their twelve-year-old twin cousins, Octavia gave a cheeky grin. "They *always* follow Grandmother's rules."

Felicity rolled her eyes, but didn't comment as she grabbed Octavia's hand and pulled her towards the small, wooden door.

With a yelp, they let go of each other's hands as a spark of static leapt between them and shot like a beam into a dark corner of the attic, where it illuminated the skirting board, reflecting off an old, discoloured gilt mirror.

Felicity gulped. "You saw that too?" she asked.

Octavia nodded mutely. Curiosity getting the better of her, she made her way across to the glittering corner.

"Tavi, don't..." Felicity whispered.

Octavia knelt, running her hands over the skirting board, where the glimmer solidified into a tiny door surrounded with climbing ivy and flowers.

"Fliss, look at this," she breathed.

Felicity hesitated, then joined her sister. "Where did that come from?" she asked, her green eyes wide.

Octavia tentatively tried to turn the miniature golden door handle.

"It's locked, but – wait, what's this?" She pointed at a miniscule scroll of parchment in front of the door. The sisters looked at each other. Just as Octavia reached out to take it, a shout echoed along the corridor and up the stairwell.

"Octavia! Felicity!"

Octavia picked up the little scroll and hastily shoved it into the pocket of her shorts, where it nestled between the moss, biscuit crumbs and doll. The sisters scrambled

to their feet in terror, running for the doorway, Octavia almost tripping over the untied lace of her trainer. They burst through it together, and Felicity paused to close the attic door firmly behind them. They tiptoed down the wooden steps into the shadowy stone corridor. Looking around, they darted into the nearest room to catch their breaths and watched dark clouds roll in over the sea, visible from the large, arched window.

Moments later, the door was flung open as a tall, austere, silver-haired woman glared into the room.

"Girls, where have you been? I have been looking the length and breadth of this Castle – and look at the state of your clothes!"

"S-sorry, Grandmother, we were playing hide-and-seek and didn't hear you," Felicity stuttered, looking sideways at Octavia and shaking her head slightly.

Their grandmother regarded them for a moment from narrowed eyes, then said, "Very well; come, it is time for tea." She paused, then added with a touch of exasperation, "Octavia, your laces are untied again."

Evelyn Bloom, the girls' grandmother, ran a tight ship and afternoon tea was at 3.30pm sharp.

When Octavia had re-tied her laces, she and Felicity meekly followed their grandmother down to the drawing room where Martha and Beatrice, their summer dresses spotless and blonde braids shining, sat at the table. They cast curious glances at their cousins, who both shook their heads.

"Later," mouthed Felicity, taking her seat opposite them.

As she passed by, Octavia patted the head of Bronwen, her Old English sheepdog, who gazed up at her with adoring eyes. Sitting down, she sneakily took a biscuit and fed it to Bronwen, who took it gently and lay down under the table, crunching on it as quietly as she could. Octavia was so glad to have Bronwen at the Castle too; it was comforting to have a piece of home with her.

Pouring tea from an ornate black and gold teapot, Grandmother speared the girls with an intense look.

"I have some news," she announced. "My sister, your Great-Aunt Clara, will be coming to stay. She has had a leak in her river boat and needs somewhere to stay whilst it is being repaired." This last sentence was uttered with a twist to the lips, as if the words had left a bad taste in her mouth. The sisters were as unalike as Octavia and Felicity were. Octavia, with her flaming tresses coming loose from her braids to wave in wisps around her heart-shaped face, was a free spirit who regularly arrived at the tea table with a smudge on her nose and a gleam in her eye. Felicity, who disliked dirt and took pride in her ebony locks, always keeping them tidy in a French braid, had a lot more in common with their older cousins.

"When will Great-Aunt Clara arrive, Grandmother?" Martha asked politely, taking an iced bun from the china cake stand. She dropped it abruptly as there came a clatter from the hall.

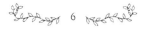

An indistinct voice muttered, "Who put that clanking suit of armour there?"

Grandmother raised her eyebrows in dismay. "I fear that should answer your question, Martha, dear." She placed her napkin upon the table and rose as a squat lady appeared in the doorway, drenched from head to toe and laden down with an odd assortment of bags. A knobbly walking stick and a gilded golden cage topped off the ensemble, the latter of which housed a red squirrel, its bright eyes fixed upon the tea table.

"You are dripping all over the Axminster carpet." Grandmother sighed.

"Oh, don't get your knickers in a twist, Evy!" Great-Aunt Clara boomed, her loud voice in sharp contrast to her diminutive size. "It's raining cats and dogs outside – not that you would notice, locked up here in your mighty fortress. And besides, it's about time this draughty old castle was brought up to date. We're nearly in 1990, for goodness' sake – it still looks like how Mummy and Daddy had it decorated in the fifties!" She aimed a wink at the four gobsmacked girls, dropped her bags, and bent to unlock the cage.

"Do not let that animal out!" hissed Grandmother, backing away, almost knocking into the table in her haste.

"Evy, you know perfectly well Rowan here is the perfect gentleman and has excellent table manners." Great-Aunt Clara gently lifted out the squirrel and placed him onto her shoulder.

Bronwen rose her shaggy head and eyed Rowan with interest. The two animals stared at each other for a moment before Bronwen gave the equivalent of a doggy shrug and laid her head back on her paws. Rowan tilted his head in apparent satisfaction and resumed his appraisal of the tea table. Open-mouthed, Octavia watched the exchange, enjoying the unexpected teatime diversion.

Taking a napkin and rubbing her frizzy, steel-grey hair dry, much to the horror of Grandmother, Great-Aunt Clara sat herself down and looked closely at the four girls.

"Well now, let me get a good look at you. I haven't seen you all since you were babies," she said, curious eyes shining. She beamed brightly. "Of course, you are Martha and Beatrice: you have the look of your dear mother Anastasia, with your golden hair."

She turned to look at Felicity and Octavia, the latter of which had gone off into a daydream, already planning to sneak off back to the attic and investigate the tiny door. Her fingers were itching to take out the little scroll and read it.

"Felicity, I would recognize your lovely raven hair anywhere. I had never seen such a shock of hair on such a small baby before." She smiled. "And Octavia – you were still in Genevieve's tummy when I came to visit, but Evy wrote to tell me you had the Blooms' fiery hair." She nodded proudly. "In every generation, up crops a little girl with copper curls. We're the magic ones," she added with a wink.

"Now, Clara, don't go filling the child's head with nonsense!" Grandmother ordered, placing a cup of steaming tea in front of her sister.

"Oh, you're cross because you had Dad's mousey hair," Great-Aunt Clara chortled, helping herself to a generous slice of carrot cake. Crumbling a piece onto a saucer, she held it up to Rowan, who nibbled delicately.

Octavia, who had been snapped out of her reverie, watched this larger-than-life character with utter fascination. Magic! She knew there was something in the air; she'd been able to feel it in her fingers ever since the miniscule, glittering door had appeared. Tingling and sparking like electricity. She had to get back to the attic!

Unable to contain her excitement, Octavia wriggled in her chair until Grandmother, irritated, snapped, "Octavia, please sit still."

Absentmindedly brushing crumbs from her lap, Great-Aunt Clara asked, with a sideways glance at her sister, "When is your birthday, Octavia? You are nearly ten, are you not?"

"Yes, I'll be ten on October the fourteenth," Octavia confirmed.

Her Great-Aunt jolted as if she'd been stung. "October the fourteenth..." she quavered. "What a coincidence." Rowan placed a tiny paw on her cheek, which had paled abruptly.

"How so?" Octavia asked, leaning forwards, confusion shimmering in her violet-blue eyes.

Grandmother stared from her sister to Octavia, then swiftly checked the tiny watch attached to her gold charm bracelet. "Is that the time? You may be excused, girls," she said in a clipped, no-nonsense voice.

Great-Aunt Clara was staring into space as the girls placed their napkins on the table and pushed back their chairs. They cast curious glances her way as they walked toward the door.

Great-Aunt Clara's voice floated behind them. "We must talk. It's time we told them—"

Octavia slowed her steps as she heard Grandmother hiss, "Not now!"

Grandmother caught up with them and ushered them from the room. "Ask Mrs Fawcett to come and clear away the tea things," she ordered, closing the door behind them with a snap.

When Beatrice had come back from speaking to Mrs Fawcett, the housekeeper, the four girls burst into a run up the wide staircase, Bronwen at their feet, sliding on the shiny flagstones as they entered the room which housed their 'secret hideout'. An ornate Chinese screen separated half of the room, which overlooked the tumbling waves. Behind the screen was an assortment of tapestry cushions and faded velvet bed throws. The girls and Bronwen threw themselves down upon them.

"What was that all about?" Felicity started, but Octavia, bursting with excitement, jumped in.

"Oh, never mind that! You'll never guess what we

found!" she directed at Martha and Beatrice.

Martha sniffed, trying to feign indifference; Beatrice looked eager, but she always wanted to please Martha, so she said nothing. Without waiting for a response, Octavia ploughed on.

"It was a tiny golden door hidden in the attic."

Martha and Beatrice exchanged looks. Octavia was renowned for having an overactive imagination.

"Tell them, Fliss! You saw it too."

Felicity nodded. "It appeared on the skirting board with little flowers woven all around it."

Vibrating with excitement, Octavia withdrew the tiny scroll from her pocket, brushed bits of moss and biscuit crumbs from it, and said, "Look, this was outside the door." The four girls bent over the scroll, heads touching, the lamplight bringing out golden flecks in their hair.

"Time is running out..." they read together. What could it mean? Bewildered, they looked at each other.

"I think we should go back to the attic and investigate," Octavia announced. The other three girls shook their heads, and Bronwen gave a grumbling growl in disagreement.

"We cannot risk Grandmother finding us," Martha vetoed. Martha, as the eldest, always tried to make the younger ones – especially Octavia – abide by the rules.

"Then we'll go at midnight, when she is sure to be asleep," Octavia said. She placed her hand in the centre, waiting. Felicity, after a moment's hesitation, placed hers on top. Martha, with a shrug, placed hers on top of Felicity's. Beatrice quickly followed suit. Bronwen added her heavy paw and, giggling, Octavia went on, "It's agreed; we'll meet in the corridor outside of our rooms at midnight. Don't forget to bring torches."

Back in her room, Octavia turned the little scroll over in her hands, mesmerised by the tiny writing, the golden ink shining. What could it all mean?

Midnight Magic

"**O**W! That was my foot!" Martha moaned, bending to rub her foot, thickly encased in pink fuzzy socks. Bronwen guiltily shuffled out of range of Martha's glare.

"Shh!" hissed Felicity, looking around the corner to check the coast was clear. The four girls and Bronwen crept along the corridor and up to the next floor towards the attic, their torches casting an eerie glow that illuminated the stone floor. Suits of armour and faded tapestries lined the walls, seeming to loom over the girls as they passed by. The girls moved closer to Bronwen at a skittering noise behind them. Pausing, they looked around for the source of the noise.

"Just a mouse," Octavia said, trying to sound

convincing as her torch picked up a small animal at the end of the corridor, but it moved too fast for her to really tell. Hastening their steps, they entered the attic. The milky moonlight barely lit up the cold attic floor, and the girls huddled together, shivering, in the centre of the room. Bronwen sniffed about and gave a little whine.

"I don't like it up here," Beatrice complained. Martha nodded in agreement and drew her robe tighter around her.

"Where was it, then?" she asked impatiently.

"Right in this corner… Oh!" Octavia broke off as the light from her torch failed to make out the door. She shone the torch over the skirting board, back and forth, but the area remained stubbornly empty.

Martha snorted in derision and raised an eyebrow at Beatrice as, in confusion, Octavia turned back to Felicity, who looked just as bemused.

How did the door appear earlier? Octavia wondered. *Did I say a magic spell by accident? Or maybe…* She remembered that it had appeared after Felicity had grabbed her hand, so she did the same now, drawing Felicity closer to the corner of the room. A warmth spread down Octavia's arm, tingling in her hand where it joined with Felicity's, and the glittering light once again shot forwards from their clasped fingers. It sparkled in the glow of the torch, revealing the golden door once again.

"There!" Octavia pointed triumphantly, turning to face Martha and Beatrice, who stood with their mouths hanging open.

"Ohhhh," said Beatrice in awe as Martha bent to get a closer look, her eyes narrowed suspiciously. "So beautiful."

The girls all started talking at once, excited and intrigued by what it could all mean. Just as their voices were getting louder, a cough echoed around the dark room. The girls all jumped, clutching at one another in fright. Goosebumps sprang up along Octavia's arms.

"I see you've discovered our family's little secret," said a voice from the shadows.

The girls turned as one, expecting to see their stern grandmother, but instead there stood their great-aunt leaning heavily on her gnarled wooden walking stick, Rowan watching beadily from his perch on her shoulder, "It's a good job that Rowan saw you were on your way up here instead of your grandmother," she said gruffly. "Oh, don't look so scared, I won't tell her; she's in denial about all this. But she can't hide from it forever," she added with a troubled look.

Gesturing to the striped couch with her walking stick, Great-Aunt Clara said, "Take a seat, girls, for I have a fairy tale to tell you all." She waited until the girls had sat, Bronwen at their feet, before settling herself upon the window seat, sending up a cloud of dust. It gave her a coughing fit that echoed around the shadowy attic. Rowan leapt from her shoulder with a reproachful look and went to stand sentry by the Fairy Door, washing himself clean.

"Before I start my tale, I'm curious to know how you discovered the door," Great-Aunt Clara said.

"We were playing hide-and-seek and Fliss found me. When she pulled me up, static shot from our hands, and there in the corner was the door," Octavia explained simply.

"Of course; the sibling bond. The door doesn't usually reveal itself to the Key Keeper before they are ten... that must be it," Great-Aunt Clara mused.

"Key Keeper?" questioned Octavia. This was getting interesting.

"I'll get to that. Now, you know our family, the Blooms, have always lived here. But what you don't know is why it is so special or why us girls always keep the Bloom name, even if we marry," Great-Aunt Clara began, her eyes shining as she leant forwards. "Hundreds of years ago, the fairy folk and us humans lived in harmony. But that all changed as humans became scared of magic and anything 'different'. When it was agreed that the doorway between the human and fairy worlds would have to be closed, our family were tasked with becoming guardians of the door and keepers of the key. The Blooms were descended from a relationship between a fairy prince and a human girl. Their twin daughters were jointly tasked with being the door's first Guardian and Key Keeper. The twin daughter with fiery hair like her fairy father became the Key Keeper, and her sister with golden locks like her mother became heir to Castle Bloom, and the Guardian to the Fairy Door hidden in its attic." She paused to let all of this sink in, the girls looking at each other with varying expressions over their faces. Martha's was of apparent disbelief, but the others turned back in excitement to listen to the rest of the tale.

Great-Aunt Clara continued, "In every generation, a girl-child is born with the same copper curls and violet-blue eyes. That child upon her tenth birthday becomes the next Key Keeper and her sister – and thanks to the fairy magic she always has one – becomes the Guardian, ready to inherit Castle Bloom when the time comes." She stopped as Octavia and Felicity turned to look at each other in disbelief.

"But I have black hair," Felicity said, unconsciously running a hand over her thick braid.

"The Guardian's hair colour is not important – it is the child with the copper curls that can become the Key Keeper. Her sister becomes the Guardian."

"But what about us?" Martha interrupted, her indignation at not being given a starring role overriding her disbelief. "We are the eldest."

Great-Aunt Clara nodded at Martha's point and said, "You become Secret Keepers, a very important role that many Blooms have inherited. Only girls in our family know of our history and with what we have been tasked. You will grow up and marry, but will, as tradition dictates, keep the Bloom name. Hopefully, you will have daughters of your own – one of which may become the next Key

Keeper."

"So, Dad doesn't know?" Octavia interrupted, wondering how she would ever be able to keep such a big secret as this from her beloved father.

Great-Aunt Clara looked torn for a moment before answering. "Well, as to that, it just so happens that both your fathers are aware of Fairy Land because of – um – well, um... Never mind about that now," she finished, looking flustered.

Octavia frowned but was prevented from asking more as Beatrice, who had been avidly listening, spoke up. "Why did *you* not marry, Great-Aunt?" she asked.

"Well, there is more to this tale, and sadly it does not have a happy ending," Great-Aunt Clara began. She opened her mouth to carry on, but a gasp at the door stopped her.

"Clara! Girls! What are you doing in here?" Grandmother stood framed in the doorway, a trembling hand pressed to her chest.

Great-Aunt Clara got guiltily to her feet. Leaning heavily on her walking stick, she turned to face her sister. "Evelyn, they were up here when I arrived... but what are *you* doing here? I thought you had vowed never to come back to the attic."

Shock and something indefinable played across Grandmother's face. "I thought I heard a noise, so I came to investigate – and it's a good thing I did. I specifically asked you not to tell the girls anything!" she accused her sister.

"They had already found the door, Evy; what could I do? Octavia will be ten soon. She would have found out then. They are not babies; we can't protect them forever," Great-Aunt Clara said sadly.

Grandmother stared at the tiny golden door, shining like a miniature star in the corner of the room. Finally tearing her eyes from it, she turned to Great-Aunt Clara.

"Genevieve will not be happy about this. How much did you tell them?"

Octavia's ears pricked at the mention of her mother, but she didn't dare interrupt this intriguing turn of events.

"Only the bare bones, but they need to know the rest!" Great-Aunt Clara replied defiantly. Grandmother shook her head.

"No, I forbid it! Girls, back to bed with you. I need to telephone Genevieve and tell her what a mess you have got us into! Not yet here twenty-four hours, and already you have thrown Castle Bloom into chaos!" Grandmother turned to shepherd the girls from the room.

"But, Grandmother, we are Blooms too. We should hear the rest of the tale," Octavia pleaded, planting her feet stubbornly on the cold stone floor.

"This isn't one of your make-believe games, Octavia, this is real, and I need to speak to your mother and aunt before it gets out of hand... again," Grandmother said, and clamped her lips firmly closed. Brooking no argument, she led the four bewildered girls firmly from the attic, followed by Bronwen, who looked puzzled by these night-time antics.

"We will talk in the morning," Grandmother threw over her shoulder to Great-Aunt Clara, who exchanged a look with Rowan. He tilted his fuzzy head and chattered keenly.

"Quite right, Rowan, I have indeed done it this time," Great-Aunt Clara told him as she followed the others from the attic. Casting one last look at the golden door gleaming on the skirting board, she closed the door behind her.

Octavia waited until Grandmother had left the bedroom before jumping out of bed and running over to slide into Felicity's.

"I knew there was something magical about that door!" she whispered excitedly. Bronwen raised her head sleepily from beside the bed, but seeing nothing to interest her, curled up again and was soon dozing.

Felicity, always the more sensible of the two, bit her lip. "But why is Grandmother so angry, and why does she need to speak to Mum?" she wondered.

"Oh, probably because Mum, with her copper hair like mine, is the current Key Keeper. She probably wanted to tell us herself," Octavia said airily, convinced nothing sinister could ever enter the candyfloss-pink world she

made her home in.

Felicity didn't look convinced, but let it go. "Your feet are freezing! Go back to your own bed," she said with a shiver.

Octavia giggled and obligingly went back to her own cosy bed, excited to see what other revelations the morning would bring.

Octavia was gliding through misty woodland, her long nightgown becoming damp with dew. Will-o'-wisps swirled with glittering fireflies to leave a flickering trail, beckoning her onward. Above the delicate web of branches overhead hung a golden crescent moon in an indigo, star-strewn sky. Octavia trailed her hand through the dandelion clocks, feeling the delicate puffs lift and dance. She smiled, thinking that they looked like fairies with tiny, shimmering wings. Fairies? She shook her head, eyes closed to the vision, but upon opening them the fairies were still there, smiling serenely at her.

"Come," they chorused, flying ahead. Octavia followed, her bare feet making no sound on the springy, moss-covered ground. Before long, they came out into a wide clearing; a still, silent pond sat in its centre. Octavia looked at the fairies, who simply pointed at the pond. Octavia tentatively walked toward the edge of the water.

She looked down to gaze at her reflection, copper waves hanging loosely around her face, her violet-blue eyes wary.

With a slight ripple, her reflection changed: a boy was gazing back at her. Copper curls tumbled messily atop a freckled face with the same eyes but with a curious gleam in their depths. He was holding out an opalescent flower which shimmered violet in the moonlight. Shocked, Octavia stepped back.

"Tavi, don't go! You need to find me! Find the key and save me!" The boyish plea echoed in her head.

Whipping around, Octavia looked for the speaker. Seeing no one, she stepped back to the water's edge. The boy was no longer looking mischievous, but scared.

"But who are you?" she whispered.

"You know who I am... Otto," the voice in her head replied. "Save me, Tavi!" The words echoed around her head. "Tavi, Tavi, Tavi..."

Octavia awoke with a jump, her heart pounding as she was roughly shaken. Felicity stood next to her bed, white-faced and shivering.

"You were having a nightmare! You kept shouting that you have to save Otto. Who's Otto?"

Octavia took a few calming breaths and sat up,

looking around. For a moment she didn't recognise the circular tower room with sea-green bed curtains and wide arched windows, where a crescent moon could be glimpsed suspended in the cloudless sky.

"I don't know," she murmured, "but it sounds familiar, like I *should* know." Octavia looked up at Felicity, who was watching her with a worried look on her face.

"Try to go back to sleep," Felicity said finally, turning to go back to her own bed and closing her rose-pink curtains against the night's chill.

Bronwen jumped up beside Octavia comfortingly as she lay back down on her side and gazed up at the moon. *Was it a dream? I'm sure I've heard the name Otto before.*

Unbidden, a memory flashed through her mind. A few months ago, she hadn't been able to sleep and had been going downstairs to get a glass of water when urgent voices had stopped her. She listened for a little longer, and realised that her mother was crying, and her father was trying to comfort her. Taking care to miss the creaky step, Octavia slowly sat down on the stairs in surprise. The idea of her usually strong mother brought to tears filled her with an uneasy feeling. She listened to her parents' conversation, worriedly nibbling on her lower lip.

"Kit, we *have* to help Otto. He doesn't have much time left," Mum was sobbing. Through the open living-room door, Octavia could see her curled up on the squishy armchair in the corner of the room.

Dad was pacing, running his hands through his thick,

black hair. "We're close, Genny, I can feel it. We need two more flowers and we'll have the cure. We have to have faith we will find them!" He stopped pacing and bent to kneel at Mum's side.

Octavia strained to hear her mother's reply and leant forward, unintentionally pressing on the creaky step. She froze for a second at the noise before quickly tiptoeing back to her room, not wanting to be caught eavesdropping. Just as she drew the covers over herself and closed her eyes, her door silently opened and, after a few breathless moments, closed again.

The next morning, she had forgotten about the strange scene she had witnessed and had thought no more about it until now. Determined not to forget this time, she resolved to find out who this mysterious boy who looked like her was.

Three

The Calm before the Storm

OCTAVIA'S ELBOW SLIPPED OFF THE TABLE as she struggled to prop herself up. Stifling a yawn, she reached for a slice of buttered toast.

"I am not surprised you are tired this morning, what with all the gallivanting you girls got up to last night. I am most disappointed in you; especially you, Martha and Beatrice – as the eldest you should be setting a better example. I had strictly forbidden you to enter the attic!" Grandmother sniffed, picking up her paper-thin china teacup.

"We are very sorry, Grandmother," said Martha, casting a furious sideways look at Octavia, who was once again staring off into space, oblivious to Grandmother's disappointment.

"Well, be that as it may, we will speak no more about it for now. I am expecting to hear back from your mother today, Felicity and Octavia. I left a message, but your parents are extremely difficult to get hold of when they are in the field," Grandmother said as she absentmindedly toyed with her gold charm bracelet. The tinkling brought Octavia out of her daydream.

"Can I speak to Mum?" Octavia, forgetting her tiredness, asked with an expectant smile. "There is so much I want to ask her!"

Grandmother pursed her lips. "I think it best if only I speak to her. We don't want to worry her unnecessarily when she is so far away."

Octavia slumped in disappointment. "May I be excused, please, Grandmother?" she asked in a small voice.

Grandmother nodded, and Octavia dejectedly walked from the room, followed by a prancing Bronwen who must have thought Octavia was headed for the kitchen. This summer holiday wasn't turning out the way Octavia had hoped. She longed for adventure, and had really thought she was on the verge of one. But no, it had been snatched away from her before it had even begun!

On autopilot, she found her feet taking her back to the attic. She stared up the steps at the closed wooden door, debating whether to go in, when a noise stopped her. Turning around, she saw Rowan sitting on the window ledge opposite, nibbling on a bright red apple.

"Oh, hello, Rowan." Octavia didn't expect a reply, and was startled when the squirrel stopped nibbling and gave her a wink.

Of course he didn't wink. Squirrels didn't wink, did they? Octavia thought and shook her head, the sleepless night must be catching up with her. Turning from the attic, she decided that curling up with a good book would be a wise way to pass the time.

A ringing awoke Octavia with a jump; the book she had been reading slid from her lap onto the library floor. She could hear a voice coming from Grandmother's sitting room. Tiptoeing over to the door, which was slightly ajar, Octavia listened but caught only mumbled words at first. Grandmother's voice become more distinct as she came closer to the door, taking a turn around the room as she talked.

"All right, dear, I will expect you tonight. What time will you be here? Oh, that late? Very well; we can discuss everything then. Goodbye."

In the silence that followed, Octavia crept back to her fallen book. *Who was Grandmother talking to? I hope it was Mum,* she thought. She hadn't seen either of her parents for nearly five weeks and was really missing them.

Octavia hid behind a bookshelf as Grandmother's

door opened. Peeping through the gap, she watched as Grandmother left the library and headed out into the entrance hall. It looked like another midnight investigation would be on tonight's agenda. She *had* to see if it was her mother who would be arriving tonight.

At dinner, Octavia was on her best behaviour. She ate her roast beef, potatoes and vegetables with no argument. Grandmother was still not in a good mood, and Great-Aunt Clara kept throwing troubled looks in her direction. Even Rowan could obviously sense a tension in the air as he cowered on Great-Aunt Clara's shoulder.

"May I show you my latest drawings, Grandmother? I captured some lovely scenes today along the coast. It was such a beautiful day with the wind whipping the waves up." Martha was desperately trying to get back into Grandmother's good graces and had been simpering and trying to please her since they'd sat down. Beatrice exchanged a grimace with Octavia, who tried hard to stifle a giggle. Felicity nudged Octavia hard in the ribs, which only caused her to draw more attention to herself.

Grandmother cast a disparaging eye over her youngest granddaughter, but turned to Martha and said, "That would be delightful. You may bring them to my sitting room after dessert. You have inherited your great-

grandfather's skill with paper and pencil – he would be most proud of you."

Martha turned a smug smile on the other girls, who inwardly groaned.

After a dessert of sticky toffee pudding, which was Octavia's favourite – and Rowan's, judging by the amount he consumed – the girls went off to spend some quiet time before bed. Martha swanned off to show her drawings to Grandmother, whilst Beatrice and Felicity headed to the library.

Octavia, feeling itchy and at a loose end, made her way up to the gallery where all her family's portraits were hung. Feeling the need to be close to her mother, she stood in front of her portrait in its gilded frame and looked up into her mother's violet-blue eyes, which were so like her own. Wondering how Mum must have felt when she had found out she would be a Key Keeper to a tiny door, Octavia examined the portrait with interest. Noting the relaxed stance and the cheeky sparkle in her mother's eyes, she decided that Mum would have taken it in her stride and relished the prospect.

Feeling comforted, Octavia turned to inspect the other portraits lining the long walls. She began to pick out all the ladies with copper curls like hers. Trailing past Cassandra Bloom then Madeleine Bloom, she stopped abruptly at Francesca Bloom and stared at the large, beautiful, jewel-coloured butterfly perched on the lady's finger. Octavia took a step back, then retraced her steps to

Cassandra's and Madeleine's portraits and narrowed her eyes at the rabbit in the first painting and deer in the next. The animals seemed almost ethereal. *I wonder...?* Octavia thought, and ran along the worn carpet, picking out other copper-haired ladies. She came to the realisation that each lady had a woodland creature either on their shoulder or standing next to them. Cunning foxes, bright butterflies, quizzical birds – quite the menagerie, it appeared.

Intrigued, Octavia pondered the portrait of a much younger Great-Aunt Clara, Rowan sitting proudly upon her shoulder. How curious.

In the painting of her mother, her pet sparrow, Pan, was perched on Mum's arm. Mum had told her she had rescued Pan when he was a fledgling. How long did birds live? Surely this couldn't be the same bird – but it certainly looked like the Pan Octavia had grown up with and played with, with the funny little tilt to his head and intelligent black eyes. Mum had to be about eighteen in this portrait. Very curious indeed.

A clunk on the floor had Octavia turning, and she saw Great-Aunt Clara walking toward her, leaning on her gnarled stick.

"Ah, I see you are putting two and two together," Great-Aunt Clara said with a pointed look at Rowan, who sat very still on her shoulder, watching Octavia with interest.

"Great-Aunt Clara! I have so many questions—" Octavia broke off as Felicity called from the gallery's

archway.

"There you are, Tavi! Mrs Fawcett has run your bath. Grandmother wants us in bed early tonight."

"In a minute – Flissy, look at this..." Octavia gestured to the portrait of their mother. "Don't you think it odd how long Mum has had Pan for?"

Felicity looked puzzled for a second. "Well, I never really thought about it. Maybe birds can live for a long time," she said with a shrug.

"Maybe," Octavia murmured, still not entirely convinced, and looked at Great-Aunt Clara, who was grinning widely.

"Come on, we don't want to give Grandmother another reason to be angry at us. She has been in such a horrible mood today." Felicity shuddered, leading the way from the gallery.

Great-Aunt Clara gestured after Felicity. "You'd better go; we don't want to upset your grandmother further. You'll find out everything soon enough."

With a frustrated huff, Octavia nodded and, after one final look into her mother's eyes, followed her sister.

Octavia lay in the dark, listening as Felicity's breathing evened out. Once she was sure her sister was asleep, she quietly slid back her bed covers and felt about in the moonlight for her slippers. With an exasperated sigh, she slid them out from where Bronwen had pillowed her head on them. Bronwen opened one sleepy eye in protest, gave Octavia's hand a lick and fell back to sleep.

Octavia knew she had to be careful not to get caught this time, so she put on her slippers on silently, pocketed her torch, and slipped from the bedroom. She paused out in the corridor, looking both ways before creeping along it. At the top of the main staircase, she peered down into the empty entrance hall. Grabbing a velvet cushion off a nearby window seat, she settled herself in the shadows to wait.

The fierce wind Martha had mentioned earlier had turned into a muggy late-summer storm; lightning zigzagged across the sky, slashing the clouds like a whip, swiftly chased by a boom of thunder that shook the castle walls. Octavia watched the raging storm visible from the large windows for a few moments and was jolted from her reverie as the front door was thrown open in a sudden gust of wind. A familiar, slight figure in a battered leather jacket and dusty biker boots fought to wrestle it closed.

"I knew it," Octavia murmured as her mother pushed the door closed and leaned against it briefly, before reaching into her jacket and pulling out Pan. The little bird flew happily around the entrance hall, stretching his wings. Octavia watched Mum walk determinedly toward the library, hefting her familiar brown leather backpack, Pan flying after her. Octavia shrank back as Mum cast a troubled look up the stairs as if she could sense her youngest daughter hiding there.

When Mum had gone into the library, Octavia raced back to her room to wake Felicity.

"Mum's here," she whispered fervently, shaking her awake.

"Wha— Octavia, what are you doing up again? You're going to get us into trouble," said Felicity, rubbing the sleep from her eyes.

"But Mum is here! I saw her going into the library. Come on." Octavia pulled her sister up and turned to race into the connecting room to wake her cousins. By the time all the girls were awake and had found their slippers, Octavia was practically vibrating with impatience.

"If we get caught, I'm saying I tried to stop you," said Martha with a yawn.

Octavia nodded indifferently and led the way to the library, with Bronwen sleepily bringing up the rear. Raised voices could be heard through the open door of Grandmother's sitting room. The name "Otto" had Octavia and Felicity looking at each other in shock.

Octavia watched through the gap in the door as her mother paced up and down the circular room, her waist-length copper braid whipping around her. Pan flew around her head like a comical cartoon bird. Throwing off her leather jacket, Mum turned to face Grandmother and Great-Aunt Clara.

"I can't believe the girls have found out like this – I

wanted to be the one to explain it all to them when we had all the flowers necessary to break the curse," she said. She stopped pacing and ran a hand across her travel-weary face. "Kit, Ana and Piers are so close to getting the Corpse Flower in Indonesia. It only blooms once a decade, so this is our only chance. It was lucky I was following another lead, albeit a false one, on the last flower, so I was close by and could get home quickly and deal with this new problem."

Grandmother tentatively put a hand on her daughter's arm. "I know this has been so hard for you, and I'm sorry I couldn't protect them. I should have kept the door to the attic locked. I assumed they would listen when I told them not to go up there." She sighed.

Mum wryly twisted her lips. "I'll guess Octavia was the ringleader."

Great-Aunt Clara said with a chuckle, "She has her mother's spirit," but stopped abruptly as her niece raised an eyebrow at her.

Octavia watched as, with a sigh, Mum threw herself onto a chair near the fire and gazed pensively into the flames.

"Mother, Aunt," she began, "I know you told me the key to the door was lost, but is there any other way of getting to Fairy Land?"

Grandmother's hand shook as she picked up the teapot to pour tea. "Why? Why would you want to? You know what happened last time."

"I know it pains you, but all the research we have done over the last nine years shows there is no such flower as the Arianthe flower – well, not in this world anyway. The trail has gone dead. I've exhausted all my leads..." Mum trailed off, letting the significance of her words sink in.

Meeting her daughter's eyes, Grandmother sighed. "You really think the last flower is in Fairy Land?"

Mum nodded, and said desperately, "It's the only way to save Otto."

Great-Aunt Clara took a sip of tea before saying, "There is no other way to get through the door; we were tasked with guarding it so that no one could go through it. In hindsight, it's probably a good job the key was lost, after all the damage that was caused last time."

Mum looked sharply at Great-Aunt Clara, who had the grace to look contrite and mumbled, "But if there is a way to save Otto, then of course you have to try."

In the silence that followed, Grandmother cast a cautious look at Great-Aunt Clara and Mum and cleared her throat. "I'm afraid I have a confession," she told them tremulously.

They both looked at her, curiosity evident in their gazes. Rowan's ears perked up in interest and Pan landed on the back of Mum's chair, watching beadily.

Setting down her teacup, Grandmother walked over to Great-Aunt Clara. "After what happened to Henry, I thought it best if the key remained lost," she said, and Octavia could see the tears shining in her grandmother's faded green eyes.

"What do you mean? The key fell out of Henry's pocket in Fairy Land. That's what we both concluded," Great-Aunt Clara said, confusion written across her face.

"We landed back in the attic, and after the two of you left to go down to the kitchen, there on the floor was the tiny key shining up at me. I took it, and I placed it on my charm bracelet so that I could ensure no one would ever go through the door again!" Grandmother finished vehemently.

Great-Aunt Clara was momentarily speechless. "But... but that was not for you to take – I was the Key Keeper, not you!"

"Yes, and my jealousy of that fact is what started all of this!" Grandmother collapsed into a chair as sobs wracked her slim frame.

Great-Aunt Clara and Mum exchanged horrified looks at this display of weakness from Grandmother, who always bore everything with an iron reserve.

"There, there; don't take on so, Evy," Great-Aunt Clara said with sympathy in her voice, and went over to rub her sister's hand. "We were both in the wrong. I lorded over you with the fact that I, the younger sister, got to be Key Keeper and not you. Look where our spite and jealousy got us; with poor Henry, and now Otto, paying the price."

"Maybe that's what needs to happen, we go full circle – this all started in Fairy Land; I have a feeling it needs to end there," said Mum musingly. "I have to try, for Otto's sake."

Outside in the library, the girls were jostling each other to hear better. Beatrice accidently fell into Octavia, who fell against the door, pushing it fully open.

"Girls!" Mum stood with her hands on her hips. "How long have you been there?"

"Long enough," Octavia said, running over to hug her mother, who squeezed her tightly for a moment before releasing her.

"Listen, there is so much you need to know, but now is not the time. You should go back to bed whilst I finish talking to Grandmother and Great-Aunt Clara."

"About Otto?" said Octavia slyly. There was a captive silence in the room as the three older ladies looked at one another in shock.

Four

The Truth Will Out

MUM NARROWED HER EYES AT OCTAVIA. "What do you know about Otto?" She addressed Grandmother and Great-Aunt Clara: "Mother, Aunt?"

They both shook their heads in confusion.

"They didn't tell me; I had a dream about him last night after we discovered the Fairy Door," said Octavia matter-of-factly.

Mum gasped. "You dreamt about him? What did he say, how did he look?" she demanded. Gripping the arm of the nearest chair, she slowly lowered herself into it.

Octavia, shocked by the sudden whiteness of Mum's face, sat on the footstool and held her hands. "Well, he looked like me, only with freckles. He said I had to find the key and save him. Oh! And he was holding out a pearly, violet flower," she remembered.

A rush of colour flooded back into Mum's face. Triumphant, she looked at her mother. "I knew it. The last flower *is* in Fairy Land!"

Grandmother's face fell in horror, and a sudden, inexplicable pang of sympathy for the older woman rose up in Octavia.

"But, Mum, why do you need the flowers?" Felicity asked, joining Octavia on the footstool.

Mum sighed; a mix of emotions waged a war across her face. She took Felicity's hand so the three of them were linked. "I didn't want any of you girls to find out like this, but I'm afraid we have been keeping a bigger secret from you." She paused and looked deep into Octavia's eyes. "We thought it was for the best to keep it hidden; we had planned for this to all be resolved years ago, but sadly that has not been the case. You should know that fairies can be tricky, and not all of them are the kind, wish-granting ones you read about in your books, Octavia."

Martha and Beatrice silently sat on the green velvet sofa next to Great-Aunt Clara, who patted them absentmindedly. Bronwen whined and went over to lick at Octavia's hand. She plunged her spare hand into the dog's thick fur for comfort.

"If we are going to tell this story, I think we need to start at the beginning," Grandmother said in resigned tones. "I am not proud of my part in this whole debacle,

but I have done my best to shelter you girls from any more danger." Taking a sip of fortifying tea, she sat in her chair. "It all started the summer when your Great-Aunt Clara turned ten; our mother and our aunt held this grand ceremony in the ballroom with all of our other of-age female relatives. Clara was made the new Key Keeper, and I am ashamed to say I was very jealous of her. I tried to take my role of Guardian seriously, but I'm afraid my jealousy got the better of me."

"It's not entirely your grandmother's fault, girls – I did show off a bit, and as siblings are wont to do, teased her about it. I felt I had always been in your grandmother's shadow and now it was my time to do something important," Great-Aunt Clara said, turning to look at her sister with an apologetic smile.

Grandmother nodded and took a deep breath. "You girls all know we had a brother, Clara's twin brother Henry – he died young, just after the end of the second world war." Her hands momentarily tightened on the arms of the chair. "Well, in my envy I told Henry about the key, which was strictly forbidden, as only females in our family are to know of the secret we guard in the attic. It was a windy day in autumn and Clara was up in the attic; she loved to sit up there, daydreaming."

Octavia shuffled uncomfortably in her seat. That sounded familiar.

Great-Aunt Clara spoke up. "I was up there practicing revealing the door. We had to know how to call it into

being in case of emergencies, and I had just run my hand along the skirting board when Henry raced in with Evy right behind him." Her usually twinkling eyes dimmed as she recounted the painful memory. "I kept the key on a piece of ribbon, and he whipped it from around my neck and threatened to open the door. He thought it was all a great lark. I tried to stop him messing about with the key, but it all happened so fast – he placed the key in the lock and before I knew it, we were all standing in a clearing in a wood." She paused before continuing. "I had tried to pull the key out from its lock, but in all of the jostling, I must have inadvertently turned it; only a Key Keeper or key-keeper-to-be would be able to turn the key," she explained. Rowan cast solemn eyes upon her pale face.

Grandmother took up the story. "In the clearing stood a fairy queen. She was beautiful, with her long dark hair and glittering black dress, but her wrath was terrifying. We had interrupted a ceremony of some sort – she was facing the enormous moon, her staff pointed at it, and speaking strange, foreign-sounding words when our arrival obviously distracted her. She was absolutely furious with us. She shouted at us that she had lost her chance to rule because the Dragon Moon only came once every 200 years. None of this made any sense to us, so we didn't know what to say. She, however, recognised us for who we were, and wanted to make us suffer. A long time ago, we Blooms had been allowed to visit Fairy Land at our leisure, hence why we still had the key, but something

had changed since then and a new Guardians' code had been put in place to keep all humans out. A code which we had just inadvertently broken.

"The evil fairy queen took her staff, and with the last vestiges of the magic from the Dragon Moon, cursed Henry and all subsequent boy babies to early deaths, making us Bloom girls watch as we lost brothers and sons." Grandmother finished the tale. "Oh, she was cruel – told us we wouldn't miss them, as it was the females who held the power."

Octavia gulped in horror as she listened, the fairy-tale adventure she longed for becoming a nightmare. Silent tears were making their way down Mum's cheeks. Great-Aunt Clara, who was also crying, blew her nose loudly, making Rowan leap from her shoulder in fright.

"Nesrin, for that was the dark fairy queen's name, left us huddled on the forest floor together, not knowing how to get back home. We weren't alone for long, as another fairy queen appeared, but this one was serene in her beauty, and light glowed from within her, illuminating the dark clearing. Her name, she told us, was Rhosyn, and whilst she could not undo the curse her sister, Nesrin, had placed upon Henry, she could offer protection and sanctuary in Fairy Land to any baby boy born into the Bloom family up until their tenth year."

Grandmother paused, her shoulders drooping as if a great weight had settled there. "Henry was ten when he was cursed, so it seemed fitting. She provided us with a recipe for a cure to reverse the curse for these subsequent babies. After they reached their tenth birthdays they would be returned to our world, where, if the curse was not broken, they wouldn't reach adulthood. Poor Henry was fifteen when he sadly perished." Grandmother, her hands shaking, took a deep drink of tea, and continued, "Rhosyn sent us back to our world with the recipe, and a small bottle of transportation dust that would allow us to send any boy babies through to her if needed. She modified Henry's memory so he had no knowledge of Fairy Land and what his fate would be. We told him that we had been playing hide-and-seek in the attic and he believed that, happily going off to the kitchen with Clara. Boys are rare in our family; Henry had been the first boy born in generations. That's why we Bloom girls keep our name in order to carry it on."

"Which leads us to Otto," Mum began, standing to pace the room once again. "Although boys are rare in our family, twins are not." She gave a brief smile to Martha and Beatrice. "Your mother already had you two girls, and I had Felicity, when I found out I was pregnant again – this time with twins."

Octavia let out a gasp. "Twins?"

Mum stopped pacing and crouched next to her. "Naturally, I assumed it would be girls. Boys were practically unheard-of. You were born first, all copper curls and flailing fists. You can imagine how surprised and horrified I felt when the doctor told me I also had

a son; I knew what his future held. Otto had the same copper curls as you but stared quietly up at me with enormous, inquisitive, violet-blue eyes. The doctors couldn't understand why I was crying so hard."

"I have a twin brother," Octavia whispered in shock. "Why did you not tell us?"

"How could we explain? It was hard enough explaining it to your father that his longed-for son would have to spend the first ten years of his life in Fairy Land unless we searched the world for rare flowers to counteract a fairy curse. He didn't believe me at first, but that all changed when we came to Castle Bloom and spoke to your grandmother. We agreed that our need was greater than keeping the secret, so I revealed the door to your father and that was enough to convince him. We decided to tell your Uncle Piers and Aunt Ana too, and the four of us made a pact to never stop looking for the flowers. The lives of all future boy Blooms were at stake." Mum looked at Octavia. "That's why we've spent so much time on research trips. We thought we would be able to use our skills and expertise and get the flowers quickly. Aunt Clara had vowed to devote her life to finding the flowers and had managed to find a couple before your aunt, uncle, father and I took over. Some of the flowers only bloom every ten to fifteen years, and that was if we could find them in the first place. We had to follow the recipe and gather the flowers in order – one for every colour of the rainbow. I have left your father, Aunt Ana and Uncle Piers to get the last flower I believe is in this world – the indigo Corpse Flower. Only the violet Arianthe flower remains, and now I know it is indeed in Fairy Land."

Octavia nodded in understanding and, determined, got to her feet. "We should go and get it. We have to help my brother."

"No! Your father and I, and your parents, too" – Mum said with a nod to Martha and Beatrice – "have this all in hand." She looked at Grandmother and Great-Aunt Clara. "I really need your support on this. I have to go through the door and get the final flower. Mother, where is your bracelet? I need the key."

"It is in a safe place; I never wear it to bed," Grandmother replied, her face pale, as she tightened the belt of her dressing gown.

Rowan started chattering, tiny squirrel paws waving in the air. Pan in response swooped down to sit at his feet, chirping in a furious manner.

"Now, now, gentlemen, I'm sure we can handle this without it coming to blows," Great-Aunt Clara admonished, her attention on the little creatures. Bronwen, with a huff at the bickering creatures, loped over to the fire and curled up.

Unnoticed by Mum and Grandmother, who were arguing over the consequences of using the key, Octavia pulled Felicity up. She motioned for her cousins to follow them and slipped from the room.

"I know where Grandmother keeps her bracelet. I'm

going to Fairy Land to save our brother," Octavia told Felicity, who vehemently shook her head.

"You can't! You heard what happened last time. What if we cause more damage? The last thing we need is more curses."

"We won't. Unlike Grandmother and Great-Aunt Clara, we know what to expect, so we'll be cautious." As she talked, Octavia was hurrying up the staircase, the three girls following. She slipped into Grandmother's room and headed to the window.

"Tavi, enough! We shouldn't be in Grandmother's room without permission," Felicity hissed, looking around uncomfortably. "I won't be a part of this!"

"Fine – I'll go alone! I only need you to help me reveal the door," said Octavia as she pushed the stone in. The secret drawer popped out from underneath the window seat once more. The other girls gasped as Octavia bent and retrieved the bracelet. Rifling through the various charms, a tingling in her fingers made her stop on a tiny golden key with a twinkling crystal embedded in its top.

"This is it," she said with certainty.

"I'll go with you," said Beatrice, finding her voice at last.

Martha turned in shock. "Bea!"

"Well, why should we let the adults have all the adventures? I'm tired of being here every holiday and Mum and Dad always being away. If we help find the cure and get Otto back, then we can go back to normal with

everyone home and together," Beatrice snapped.

Octavia held her breath as Martha and Felicity exchanged a look.

"I do miss being with Mum and Dad..." Martha agreed, trailing off. Felicity nodded slowly.

Sensing that the tides had turned, Octavia silently placed her hand in the centre between them. Felicity paused before placing hers on top, followed by Martha and Beatrice.

With no time to change clothes, the girls headed straight for the attic in their slippers and dressing gowns.

"Beatrice!" hissed Martha. "They'll hear us."

Beatrice, who had crashed into an old jumbled suit of armour, looked contrite. "Sorry, I didn't see it."

Ignoring the twins' bickering, Octavia took a deep breath and held her sister's hand. The beam of light once again shot from their clasped hands and solidified into the Fairy Door. Taking the tiny key in her damp fingers, Octavia slowly inserted it into the glowing keyhole. Time stood still as on a collective breath, she turned the key, and with a click the tiny door swung open. Rainbows, the scent of damp woodland, and the slightest tinkling of bells entered the musty attic.

Barking and the sound of running feet spurred the girls into action. Felicity grabbed Martha's hand, and she tightly gripped Beatrice's. All four turned to the attic door, as Mum, breathless, burst through it, her hand outstretched.

"Girls, no—!"

Octavia locked eyes with those of her frantic mother before a sensation of being enveloped in a thick bubble overwhelmed her. Bronwen's barking grew fainter as in a wink they were standing in a mossy clearing, and Mum and Castle Bloom were gone.

Five

Through the Door

A SHOUT ECHOED FROM THE DISTANCE, bouncing around the girls as they stood grouped in a circle of glossy red toadstools.

"Intruderzzzzz!" a thousand voices buzzed, as a swarm of bees headed toward the girls.

"Key Keeper, run!" shouted a squeaky girlish voice as a tiny grey mouse scampered across Octavia's slipper. Octavia leapt from the fairy ring, her sister and cousins following, and headed for the wood in front of her, illuminated by the large almost-full moon above. They slid into the cover of the trees as the bees chased them. Abruptly, the swarm stopped as if an invisible barrier held them back.

"We'll be safe in here; Queen Nesrin's bees cannot

enter Rhosyn's Woods," a voice squeaked near Octavia's left ear.

Octavia jumped in shock; in the corner of her eye she saw the grey mouse sitting on her shoulder.

"Do not be alarmed, Key Keeper – I am Ferren, your companion. Although I did not expect to be paired with you so soon. You have not yet reached ten human years, have you?" The little mouse twitched her whiskers as she talked. "It was so strange – I was at home in the woods when I felt this tingling in my whiskers and a strange sensation that I needed to be here at the toadstool ring. All of a sudden, you four girls appeared with a pop!"

Bemused, the four girls looked at each other, then back to Ferren.

"Companion?" Octavia asked.

"Surely you know about the Key Keepers' companions?" Ferren squeaked in surprise.

Octavia mutely shook her head, but her attention was turned to the angrily buzzing swarm of bees, hovering just beyond the treeline.

"What do the bees want?" Felicity asked, casting a wary glance at the swarm.

"They are Nesrin's alert system. She'll know you are here soon enough. We need to go deeper into the woods." Ferren leapt from Octavia's shoulder onto a fallen tree, where a sleepy toad opened one eye.

"Oh marvellous, humans! There goes my peace and quiet," the toad croaked grumpily.

"That is no way to welcome our guests, Lyffy," Ferren admonished him.

Lyffy regarded the girls with a steady green-and-golden-eyed gaze. His skin was mottled with golden spots across his jade-green skin. "Guests?" he said, one webbed hand gesticulating. "What about the code?"

Ferren tilted her head, her whiskers twitching. She turned to the girls. "Oh yes, the code! It is not safe for you to be here. Come, let's go further into the woods to talk."

"Um, excuse me, um, Ferren," Octavia stumbled over her words, "how can we understand you?"

The other three girls crowded around, eager to hear Ferren's answer.

"You are in Fairy Land now; creatures, fairies and humans can talk freely. When you become Key Keeper on your tenth birthday, I will be your companion in the human world and you, you alone, will be able to understand me there. But I will tell you more once we are safer in the woods," Ferren told her.

"Well, that explains Great-Aunt Clara's Rowan, and Mum's Pan!" Octavia exclaimed, finally understanding the funny little conversations her mother and the sparrow always appeared to be having. Octavia had just thought Mum had been playing around.

Leaving Lyffy to his solitude, the girls followed Ferren deeper into the woods. They crossed a rustic bridge, which hovered over a glittering stream. Rainbow-coloured fish leaped from the water, bubbles rising to the surface in their wake. As they popped, the most delicious scents filled the air: strawberry, blueberry and blackberry. The girls breathed in deeply, a calm stealing over them.

"Oh no, I forgot! Don't breathe in the aromas; they will intoxicate you and you will forget where you are. I am not used to dealing with human frailties," Ferren fretted, nibbling on Octavia's earlobe until she came out of her trance enough to listen to the mouse. "This way – quickly."

Octavia blinked, trying to dispel the cotton-wool feeling in her head. Sleepily, she pulled the reluctant Felicity, Martha and Beatrice along behind her until they came into a clearing. She looked around. *Where am I?* she thought in confusion. Ferren gave a squeak and thrust a sprig of leaves which smelled strongly of peppermint at the girls.

"Chew this; it will make you feel better," the little mouse told them.

Dubiously, the girls looked at the leaves. Octavia, feeling like she was in another dream, ripped a piece off, stuffed it into her mouth, and chewed. Instantly she felt back to normal and remembered where she was.

"It's fine," she told the others. Copying Octavia, the faces of the others cleared from their previous dreamy expressions back to ones of bewilderment and slight worry.

"What was that?" Octavia asked Ferren. "I forgot why I was here!"

"The Stream of Dreams – different scents give

different dreams. The dream fairies use them in their potions. They process them into sleep dust, which they sprinkle over human children to give them sweet dreams. Unfortunately, if humans inhale the pure scents for too long, they forget everything," Ferren explained apologetically.

"But how do the fairies get the dust into the human world? I thought the Key Keepers kept the door between the worlds locked."

"That is to keep the humans out of Fairy Land, not the other way around. Humans started to become afraid of our magic and slowly, over time, stopped believing, causing fairy doors all over the human world to disappear. This happened until only one remained – the one in Castle Bloom, in the care of the last family who still truly believe and who themselves have vestiges of magic running through their veins, courtesy of their fairy prince ancestor. Well, he was actually king at one point, but he passed the crown to his sister instead so he could marry a human girl!" Ferren paused, her eyes turning misty as if she was moved by the romantic notion. She twitched her whiskers before continuing. "The dream fairies and tooth fairies are still permitted to visit the human world, under cloak of darkness and to sleeping children only. Queen Rhosyn has a portal in her castle which she uses to send fairies through your door to do their nightly work. Your job as Guardian and Key Keeper is to keep the door, the last of its kind, safe: you are tasked with ensuring no human enters through it." Ferren suddenly sat up on her hind legs, her intelligent black eyes flashing. "Which brings me to ask – what exactly are you four doing here?"

Octavia exchanged looks with the other girls. "We have come to rescue my twin brother, Otto. We need to find a flower so we can make the cure and free him from the curse Nesrin has placed upon the boys in our family." She paused. "Have you seen Otto? Do you know where he is?"

Ferren twitched her whiskers. "I have heard whispers of a human boy being kept in Queen Rhosyn's castle. It is on the other side of Rhosyn's Woods."

Octavia stood up, the others following suit. "Will you take us there, please, Ferren?" she asked.

"You can't just go into Castle Enfys; you have to speak to one of Queen Rhosyn's advisors first," said Ferren. "These are dark times. Nesrin's powers are growing stronger by the day, and there are rumours she wants to control all of Fairy Land." She shivered.

"Can you take us to one of her advisors? Please, Ferren." Felicity knelt next to the little mouse, who turned her troubled black eyes her way.

After a moment's hesitation, Ferren nodded. "I will take you to see Feargal. He will know what to do."

Fireflies flitted through the trees as the girls followed Ferren through a winding trail that glittered with luminescent toadstools and night-blooming flowers. Octavia studied these flowers keenly as she passed by,

looking for the one she had seen in her dream. None matched, she realised with dismay.

"I'm cold and hungry," Martha moaned. "How much farther?" she asked Ferren.

Ferren stopped. Beyond her, the trees had thinned out to reveal a shallow valley, and nestled up on a cliff was a pearly-white castle. The moonlight illuminated it like a spotlight. "We're here," she squeaked.

Martha apparently forgot her hunger and tiredness as she gazed up at the magnificent castle, her mouth dropping open.

"Who goes there?" an imperious voice barked. A large red fox slunk out from the shadows to stand in front of Ferren and the girls.

"It's me, Feargal – Ferren – and these are the Bloom girls," Ferren announced grandly.

"More Bloom girls?" Feargal sneered. "What disaster will befall us this time?"

The others shifted uncomfortably, but Octavia met Feargal's gaze steadily and said, "We are not here to cause any trouble. We only want my twin brother back."

Feargal's eyes turned thoughtful.

"Indeed. Wait here," he commanded, racing down the valley and disappearing over the crystal bridge at the bottom. The girls watched for some minutes, but as there was no sign of his return, they sat on a few overlarge toadstools to wait.

"I know *your* name, of course, Octavia – there was

much celebration in Fairy Land when the dream fairies came back from Castle Bloom one night with the news that the next Key Keeper had been born – but I don't know your names," Ferren said, smiling at the other girls, who introduced themselves.

They passed a few pleasant minutes talking about Pan and Rowan, whom Ferren had heard about from her time at her Companion Class at Fairy School. There she had learned all about the human world and how to be a good companion to the next Key Keeper.

"So, how exactly does being a companion work?" Octavia asked thoughtfully as she toyed with the tiny golden key still nestled tightly in her palm. It was so small, it would be easy to lose it. Looking around, she plucked a strong vine from a tree trunk and twisted it into a necklace. Slipping the key onto it, she placed it around her neck and securely knotted it.

"Well, in a nutshell, I'm here to keep your belief in Fairy Land strong – a visual reminder of the bond between the Blooms and the fairy folk. Oh, and to ensure you do not use the key unless it's an emergency," Ferren finished with a twitch of her whiskers as she turned her small black eyes on Octavia.

Octavia giggled nervously. "Saving my brother is an emergency, isn't it?" she asked, tucking the key out of sight under her dressing gown.

Ferren's gaze turned thoughtful, but she looked up as Beatrice gave a shout.

"What is that?" Beatrice was pointing to something large and round glimmering in the moonlight, heading their way.

"That would be your transportation," a snide voice replied, making the girls jump. Feargal had returned silently without them noticing.

He led the way to the huge bubble, which was gently hovering above the mossy ground. Its surface had an almost mirror-like sheen. "Step inside," he instructed.

Taking a deep breath, Octavia stepped up to the bubble. Her pale face gazed back at her, slightly distorted by the curved surface. She placed one slippered foot into the bubble. Reassured that it wasn't about to pop, she pushed the rest of her body through. Surprised to find little cushioned seats inside, she helped Felicity, Martha and Beatrice climb aboard before sitting down. Ferren jumped though the bubble and came to sit on Octavia's shoulder. Feargal boarded last, and the girls gasped as the bubble slowly rose and headed toward the castle.

Octavia watched in wonder as the moonlight lit up a cascading waterfall below; rainbows bounced from the surface where the tumbling waves met the river. The bubble skimmed by the castle walls and headed for a golden platform high up on the tallest tower, where it came to a gentle rest.

The girls stood up, and Feargal motioned them to disembark. They found themselves surrounded by a crowd of fairies, who were slightly bigger than the girls in size.

The fairies stared at them inquisitively and the girls gazed back; in their dressing gowns and slippers, they were a stark contrast to the shimmering fairies. The fairytale folk that surrounded them were dressed in glittering gauzes and iridescent silks, with wings of varying size and shape, reminiscent of butterflies and dragonflies. Except for the wings, their pointed ears, and the unusual colours of their eyes and hair, Octavia could almost have believed they were human.

"Why are you so big?" Beatrice blurted out. "I imagined that you would be tiny to fit through the door."

The crowd of fairies tittered and smiled indulgently at one another.

"It is not we who are big, it is you who are small," a beautiful fairy with teal hair shot through with one copper streak remarked. She looked to be about twenty years old. "When you come through the Fairy Door, you shrink to fairy size. Fairy Land is its own miniature world, except with magic." She smiled gently. "My name is Evony. I will escort you to Queen Rhosyn." She turned to reveal a shimmering pair of rainbow wings, in between which nestled a quiver of arrows. Octavia thought her wings resembled the wings of a butterfly in shape and was utterly fascinated.

The girls followed Evony through an archway of marble and along a corridor to a grand glass staircase; she led them down it and into a glittering throne room. Three crystal thrones were placed at the far end of the room in

front of a wall of shining windows. On one of the thrones sat an elegant fairy, a crystal crown threaded through with multicoloured flowers atop her tumbling copper curls. A snow-white hare sat at her feet, its lavender eyes watching the girls keenly. As the fairy rose, her dazzling gown billowed around her, changing from green to purple to blue with its opalescent sheen. Her enormous butterfly-shaped wings extended, revealing all the colours of the rainbow.

Ferren squeaked in awe from Octavia's shoulder and whispered in her ear, "I have never been this close to the queen before."

The queen turned her benevolent gaze upon the group and smiled softly before saying, "Welcome, all, to Castle Enfys. I see you have met my daughter, Princess Evony. I am Queen Rhosyn." Her voice had a musical lilt to it which rose and fell like a song.

Evony smiled and went to stand by her mother. "These are the human girls Feargal found in your woods," she told her.

"And what would four human girls be doing in my woods?" Queen Rhosyn's purple eyes roved over Octavia's copper hair with curiosity. "It has been an age since another human girl with copper hair thought it wise to come through our door. That did not end at all well," she mused.

"Please, your majesty, I am Octavia Bloom, and this is my sister Felicity. We and our cousins Martha and

Beatrice have come to help free my twin brother Otto."

Martha tried to give a wobbly little curtsey, but her dressing gown spoiled the effect. Blushing, she straightened awkwardly, not meeting Octavia's amused gaze.

Queen Rhosyn opened her mouth to speak when a crack rent the air. Evony immediately grabbed her bow and slid an arrow from her quiver, placing herself in front of her mother.

"Guards!" she screamed as a black cloud materialised in the centre of the room.

Ferren scampered from Octavia's shoulder and down her arm in fright. Octavia scooped the mouse up and placed her safely in her pocket. A figure stepped from the cloud, holding aloft a black staff, a silver star shining at its top.

"Hello, sister dear," a sinuous voice said lazily.

The cloud cleared to reveal a haughty-looking fairy in a dress of black net, cunningly worked to appear as if it had been sprinkled with a thousand glittering stars. A silver crown sat upon her black locks, a tangle of vines and stars, and a black raven was perched on her shoulder, beady-eyed and poised for attack.

Queen Rhosyn stepped from behind Evony, who didn't lower her bow. "What brings me this pleasure, Nesrin?" she asked in a voice that said it was anything but a pleasure. "We have an agreement that you are not to enter this castle."

Fairy and animal guards filed into the room to form a circle around Nesrin, who smiled tightly. "My bees told me there were human trespassers, so I came to investigate. That is the only reason I am here – in *our* parents' castle – of course." Her silver eyes fell upon the four girls, who had banded together in fear. She sniffed as if she had caught a scent, and her eyes lingered briefly on Beatrice, who shrank against Martha. Ferren squeaked nervously from Octavia's pocket.

"No trespassers; they are here as my honoured guests," Queen Rhosyn replied smoothly, walking to stand next to the girls.

"Guests?" Nesrin spat. "You know no human is to set foot in Fairy Land, as stated in the Guardian's Code."

"A code you insisted on, and which I agreed to if you would cease your endless, futile quest at trying to rule. But now, I think it is time we revised the code. Time has passed, and humans are evolving – they are so much more accepting now; they pose no danger to us or our realm," Queen Rhosyn said calmly.

"You are a fool to believe that!" Nesrin whirled to face Octavia. "I remember your silly grandmother and her siblings. They paid dearly for breaking the Guardian's Code, and I suggest you return to your world before I curse you too!"

"You have no power in this castle," Queen Rhosyn, her voice like steel, reminded her sister. "Now go!"

"Maybe not, but they can't stay in this castle forever!"

 63

Nesrin said, and gave a taunting laugh, her attention still focused on Octavia. "You'll never break the curse, little girl; I know what you need, and it is well guarded!"

With that parting shot and an intricate movement of her staff, her black cloud reappeared. She stepped onto it and was gone.

Six

Castle Enfys

QUEEN RHOSYN TURNED TO LOOK AT THE GIRLS. "Now Nesrin knows you are here, she will do all she can to thwart any efforts to rescue your brother. She won't give up easily. She was so enraged when your grandmother interrupted her attempt at garnering more power from the Dragon Moon's magic. Using the last vestiges of the moon's power, she invoked an ancient curse. But I knew what would work as a cure. I had always made sure to study antidotes and cures, as my sister took a great interest in curses and dark magic when we were growing up." The queen looked troubled. Her eyes, so similar to Octavia's, narrowed. "If you are here, then that means you have the other flowers?" she asked.

As Ferren popped her head out of Octavia's pocket to

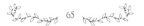

listen, Octavia nodded. "Yes; my father is hopefully getting the sixth flower as we speak. I had a dream about Otto – he was holding out a pearly purple flower, which my mother has told us is the seventh and final one needed in the cure," she explained earnestly, twisting her primrose-yellow dressing-gown belt in her hands.

Queen Rhosyn smiled. "Of course – the Arianthe flower. Yes, it is the most important part of the cure. I wondered how long it would take before a Bloom realised they would need to come back through the door to find it. The other flowers are of course found in the human world – my small attempt at giving you Blooms a head start in finding the cure." She paused. "You dreamt of your brother, you say? But that is not possible, unless..."

She trailed off, raising an eyebrow at Evony, who asked, "Shall I bring Alora to you, Mother?"

Queen Rhosyn nodded and dismissed her guards. Watching as they filed from the room, she addressed the girls. "Where are my manners?" she exclaimed, and with a flick of her globe-topped staff, shot out a rainbow. It twisted and rippled like a ribbon out of the door. Within moments, a plump fairy rushed in with a curtsey. With a flick of her own amber-stone-topped wand, a table appeared, laden with fruit, bread and a yellow-coloured liquid in glass goblets.

"Please, sit and refresh yourselves," Queen Rhosyn told the girls, who gratefully fell upon the food and drink with gusto. "Try the chamomile tea; it is most calming,"

she added, taking a cup for herself.

Octavia placed Ferren on her shoulder, and the mouse squeaked as the queen turned her luminous gaze upon her.

"Ah, I see your companion found you. I knew she would be a good fit. Your tutor was most complimentary about you, Ferren Mouseling," Queen Rhosyn said with a smile.

"Oh! The queen knows my name!" Ferren squeaked in happiness, clutching her tiny paws together, her black eyes rounded in amazement.

Everybody laughed. Octavia felt an immediate connection with this creature, and knew they were going to have lots of fun together.

"You wanted to see me, Your Majesty?" a tinkling voice asked. The girls turned to see a small fairy with pink hair and a silver dress approach the table. Her silver-veined wings fluttered anxiously.

"Yes, Alora," the queen replied, setting down her acorn-shaped cup. "Tell me, have you visited Castle Bloom recently and given the youngest Bloom daughter here one of your special dreams?" A comforting warmth spread through Octavia's back as Queen Rhosyn placed a slight hand upon her.

Alora's eyes darted from the queen to Octavia apprehensively. "It was an accident, Your Majesty. I was taking a batch of dreams to the storage room when one dropped and rolled under a door. The guard outside the

door was dozing, so I looked underneath the door to retrieve it. I could see a human boy asleep on the bed, shrouded in sleep mist. The dream bottle was open, so I quickly grabbed and recorked it." She licked her lips nervously. "I didn't tell anyone about the boy, I promise."

Queen Rhosyn looked thoughtful. "Hmm, so did Otto dream of you whilst you dreamt of him, I wonder?" She looked at Octavia musingly. "What happened to the dream bottle you dropped?" she asked Alora.

"Something told me to take it with me when I went through the door to the human world. I hadn't planned to give any dreams to the Bloom girls that night, but I felt compelled to give that particular dream to the girl with hair like yours," Alora said, eyes darting back and forth between Octavia and the queen. "I hope that was all right!"

"Well, that settles the matter; it was meant to be. The quest for the flower is indeed yours," Queen Rhosyn said, and with a nod, excused Alora. With curious eyes, Alora backed out of the room.

"Queen Rhosyn, may we see Otto?" Octavia enquired politely, after she had eaten her fill of honey-smothered bread.

"I am afraid that as part of the pact to keep him safe, he has been placed in an enchanted sleep until the cure can be created. I had to keep him hidden from Nesrin, so the fewer who knew where he was, the better," Queen Rhosyn said. "You have a busy day ahead of you, so I suggest you retire for a few hours." She stood and addressed her white hare. "Eira, please bring Briar and Sorrel to me."

The hare bounded out of the room, and swiftly returned with whom Octavia guessed to be two forest fairies.

"Please take our guests to the Amethyst room and provide them with something more suitable to wear," Queen Rhosyn requested of them.

Briar, with her brown dress and green wings, gave the illusion of falling leaves as she flew toward to girls. Sorrel, in a grass-green gown and mushroom-coloured wings, flitted over gracefully with a smile. Both had curling nut-brown hair.

Though disappointed that her attempt to see Otto had been thwarted, Octavia smiled politely at the two fairies. She and the other girls followed Martha's example and tried curtsies of their own. The queen's eyes twinkled as she inclined her head at their wobbly efforts before they left with Briar and Sorrel.

Castle Enfys was as exciting to Octavia as Castle Bloom was, although for completely different reasons. The fairy castle was filled with chattering fairies and creatures busily going about their business. Rainbow bubbles burst from circular windows as more fairies were transported in, carrying baskets of flowers and loops of vines.

"You have arrived at the right time; we are preparing for the Late Summer Night Ball – it is the most important event in our fairy calendar!" Briar told the girls, gesturing to the mounds of flowers and vines being woven into

intricate banners by a team of fairies and hummingbirds.

"When does it take place?" Martha asked, watching with interest. Her fingers twitched, and Octavia thought she was probably itching to draw the scene.

"Two nights hence – there will be a grand ball, a feast, and a ceremony to bring blessings for the new season," Sorrel explained.

The girls passed through the hall and up glass steps that chimed as they walked upon them. The fairies led them into a circular room, whose walls glittered with amethyst crystals and golden seams. The four girls were momentarily struck speechless; even Ferren's eyes grew impossibly rounder as Octavia gently placed her down on a padded seat.

"Please make yourselves at home. Oh! Let me help you get changed…" Briar remembered. Taking a twig-like wand intricately carved with leaves and thorns, topped with a green crystal, Briar waved it delicately over the four girls. In an instant, the girls' nightdresses and dressing gowns were transformed into the softest brown leggings and colourful tunics. Upon their feet, instead of fluffy slippers, were pointed leather shoes which tied like ballet slippers. Octavia wore a sunny yellow tunic, Felicity wore emerald green, Martha's was in hues of pink, and Beatrice was in blues the colour of the sky. Their hair had been expertly braided and threaded through with matching flowers, tied with strong vine.

"Wow!" said Beatrice, doing a twirl, and even Martha

looked impressed.

"Please rest," said Sorrel. "We will come to collect you for breakfast." She and Briar left the room, closing the door behind them.

Felicity, Martha and Beatrice walked over to the large, semi-circular canopied bed and lay down, the night's adventures taking their toll. They were asleep as soon as their heads hit the cloud-like pillows.

Octavia was too excited to sleep; she walked across the purple-veined marble floor to stare out of the crystal window. Ferren scampered after her and jumped onto the window seat.

"Key Keeper, you really should try to rest – as the queen said, you have a busy day and a difficult journey ahead of you," Ferren said earnestly.

"But there's too much to think about!" said Octavia. "What did Nesrin mean by 'it is well guarded'?" she asked.

"I do not know. The flowers in Fairy Land belong to everyone, but you speak of the rarest flower here – the Arianthe Flower. It blooms in the moonlight of the Late Summer Moon. I do not know where, but our flower fairies are sure to know," Ferren said, stifling a yawn.

Octavia smiled with affection at the mouse. "You should go to sleep too." She leaned her head against the window, mulling over Ferren's words. She couldn't wait for morning to come and for their quest to start; Otto's future depended on it.

A warm shaft of sunlight slowly woke Octavia from a deep sleep. She opened her eyes to find that she was still nestled on the window seat with Ferren curled up next to her, sleeping. Standing, she stretched and noticed that her sister and cousins were still fast asleep. In her soft leather shoes, she tiptoed over to the huge wooden door, pulled it open and peered out into the hallway. The hustle and bustle of the night's activities had ceased, and a silence lay over the castle.

Octavia made her way back down the musical glass steps into the wide entrance hall. It looked beautiful, festooned with glowing, shimmering flowers the like of which Octavia had never seen. Butterflies and hummingbirds fluttered from flower to flower, sipping upon nectar.

Octavia carried on down the corridor. In her storybooks, fairies stayed up late busily working and liked to sleep in; she wondered if there might be some truth to it, as she didn't come across any fairy or other creature. At the end of the corridor she came once again to the throne room, which was now empty. She had hoped to stumble across Otto's room, but even though she had known it probably wouldn't be that easy, she still wanted to see him – it was all so frustrating.

As she turned back, a shimmer out of the corner of

her eye caught her attention. An old fairy was standing in the great hall's entranceway; she beckoned Octavia over.

"You are Otto's sister?" she asked, to which Octavia nodded. "Good – you got my note."

Octavia was perplexed. "Note?" she queried.

The old fairy's crinkled wings flapped feebly against her dress of sage green, and she pushed her braid of faded green hair over her shoulder. "Yes, yes, the scroll I sent through the door telling you time was running out," she said impatiently.

"It was you? I wondered who sent it," Octavia said, looking around furtively. They were alone. "Can you take me to Otto?"

"Yes, that's why I'm here – I have looked after Otto since he arrived. I'm Hevva, a healing fairy." She gave a crooked bow. "Follow me."

Octavia's heart started beating faster. This was it! Finally, she would get to meet her brother. She followed Hevva eagerly.

Hevva took her up a winding staircase and stopped halfway up at a closed door, in front of which was a dozing badger. His striped head was bowed over as he snored deeply; he was dressed in the rainbow tabard of Queen Rhosyn's guard.

"Aloysius – useless guard," Hevva grunted, skirting past him. "Drinks too much rosehip wine."

She took a crystal key out of her pocket and inserted it into the lock; the door swung open to reveal a tall room with walls coloured the softest hues of green. A hazy mist surrounded the canopied bed, where a sleeping boy lay.

"Otto!"

Octavia started forward but Hevva held her back, her grip surprisingly strong.

"Do not enter the enchanted mist, or you too will fall into a deep sleep," she warned.

Octavia nodded and approached cautiously, careful to stay out of the mist's perimeter. She studied her sleeping brother's peaceful, freckled face as he lay still upon the green, embroidered coverlet, copper curls tumbled messily atop the pillow. If he were to open his eyes, Octavia knew they would be violet-blue like her own.

"I needed you to see him, to know what you are fighting for – but to give you words of warning also." Hevva lowered herself into a solitary rocking chair, her wings fitting through the gap in the back. "I was nursemaid to Rhosyn and Nesrin when they were girl-fairies. Rhosyn was always fair and wanted what was best for Fairy Land, but Nesrin was always jealous of her older sister. She craves power and will stop at nothing to get what she desires. You need to be careful, and please don't underestimate her." Hevva picked up a ball of silvery yarn and some long, twig-like needles and started to knit.

Octavia followed the mesmeric clicking of the twig-needles and took a deep breath. "I will do what I can to save Otto, but I will be careful too."

Hevva studied her over the rim of her green glasses

and nodded. "It was always for you to finish, girlie; your brother needs to be back in the human world with his family. I have done what I can to help him grow and thrive, but this dream-like existence is not good for humans."

Octavia turned at the sound of rustling on the stairs, and a voice said sternly, "Aloysius, are you sleeping at your post again?"

Hevva gave a husky chuckle and carried on with her knitting. She started singing a haunting lullaby as Octavia took one last look at her sleeping twin and left the room, closing the door softly behind her.

Briar fluttered above the steps with her hands on her hips, glaring at the badger, who hung his head abashedly.

"There you are, Key Keeper; the others are waiting for you." Briar turned and fluttered down the stairs with Octavia following behind her thoughtfully.

Briar led Octavia once again into the throne room, which was now set with a long table. Fairies and creatures from the fairy court all sat together breaking their fast with juicy berries, domed cakes and bread smothered in honey. Watchful eyes followed Octavia as she walked to the head of the table, where Queen Rhosyn sat. Octavia curtsied and was gratified when she didn't wobble this time. She sat next to Felicity, who gave her an exasperated sigh. Octavia gave her an apologetic look in return for disappearing. Martha and Beatrice sat opposite them, looking most at home amongst the fairy folk with their elfin features and shining hair.

Queen Rhosyn stood and tapped her staff on the table; a rainbow soared from its globe. The chatter died immediately as all eyes focused on the queen.

"We have esteemed guests joining us today from the human world. The Bloom family have kept the door to our realm safe for hundreds of their mortal years," she began, with a dazzling smile to the girls. "They have come to us for aid on a most important quest. You are all familiar with the tale of how my sister placed a curse on their menfolk many years ago, but now is the time to break that curse. We need the bond between human and fairy to be stronger than ever," she finished with a determined look. The assembled fairy court broke out into rapturous applause and stamps of hoofed feet.

Queen Rhosyn asked, "Guards, who amongst you will assist our friends in this endeavour?" Every single guard in the room stepped forward. Queen Rhosyn nodded with pride. "You serve your queen well." She perused the guards in front of her. "Aurus, I choose you."

A large golden stag stepped forward and bowed his head; his magnificent antlers brushed the floor. Rainbow bands encircled his lower legs.

"Mother." Evony put her hand on the queen's arm. "May I put myself forward to accompany them? I have been training hard – I know I am ready."

Queen Rhosyn turned her intense violet gaze on the princess. "You, daughter? Your aunt in her own domain will be a formidable foe. I cannot risk my heir, my only

child, getting hurt."

"Please, Mother, let me prove myself. If I am to be a great ruler, I need to show I can indeed protect our people," Evony pleaded.

A ripple ran through the assembled crowd at Evony's defiance.

Aurus stepped forward. "If you please, Your Majesty, I have overseen Princess Evony's training myself – she will make a great warrior," he boomed, inclining his great head respectfully.

Queen Rhosyn weighed up his words and gave a resigned sigh. "Very well, my daughter, you may go."

Evony bowed to her mother before turning to smile at the girls. Octavia returned the smile with enthusiasm; the adventure was about to begin.

Sitting, the queen addressed them, "Please eat and drink your fill; your quest begins in a few hours." All four Bloom girls exchanged looks. Only Octavia's was filled with excitement.

Seven

The Journey Begins

AFTER A BREAKFAST OF MORE HONEY CAKES and blackberries, Octavia, Felicity, Martha and Beatrice headed to the royal gardens to meet up with Haf, a flower fairy.

Bright sunlight greeted them as they followed Briar and Sorrel along the winding path that led to Haf's hut. It looked like an oversized acorn, with the stem as a chimney. Purple smoke billowed from its tip.

Briar knocked the flower-shaped knocker and called out, "Haf! We have visitors for you."

The door was flung open to reveal a tiny fairy. Her dress resembled petals of differing colours and her wings reminded Octavia of a hummingbird, shimmering and frantic.

"Visitors!" Haf trilled, clapping her hands. "Come in, come in," she said, ushering them inside. The hut's appearance was deceptive; inside was a roomy workshop with vials, bottles and seedlings arranged haphazardly on a long workbench which encircled the whole room. A sleeping nook was nestled in the rafters, and a firepit in the centre of the room sat beneath a large copper cauldron, from which the purple smoke was issuing.

"Would you like some violet tea? It is just about brewed." Haf motioned to the cauldron.

"I'm sorry, Haf, but this is not a social call – these are the Bloom girls from the human world. The queen requests that you tell them all you know about the Arianthe flower," Briar said.

Haf visibly shrank back, her vibrating wings slowing. "The Arianthe flower?" she said with a gulp. "I have never seen it, nor have any of the other flower fairies. We only know what has been passed down through the generations. Wait – I will get the book!"

She flew over to a bookcase and pulled out a heavy leafbound book.

"Every flower in Fairy Land is in this book; some flowers have pages, but the Arianthe flower has but one paragraph. Here." She turned to the relevant page and held it out for the girls to see. Ferren jumped from Octavia's shoulder to sit on the edge of the book to get a closer look.

Arianthe Flower: a violet flower with pearl sheen.

Blooms in the beam of the Late Summer Moon from a wyvern egg; must be plucked immediately or will wither and lose its magical properties. Found in the misty marshes of the North.

"What is a wyvern?" Martha asked Haf tremulously.

Haf shuddered. "That is why no living flower fairy has seen the Arianthe flower. None have been brave enough to face a wyvern; they are two-legged dragons that are fiercely protective of their eggs. Arianthe flowers are extremely rare. A wyvern needs to have eaten one of its seeds in order to lay an egg from which the next flower will bloom. And it will only bloom once a year, in the light of the Late Summer's Night Moon," she explained.

Octavia studied the short sentences and accompanying illustration, which depicted a large flower with pointed purple petals and a thick stalk sprouting from the pearly remains of a large shell.

"We have no choice; we have to collect this flower, and time is running out." Octavia met Haf's blue eyes. The fairy gave a squeak of dismay.

"It is not safe! The only fairy to have seen the flower, the one who wrote this description in the book, came back gravely wounded. His warning has been passed down from fairy to fairy." Haf clasped her hands together, imploring them to change their minds.

"We need it to save my brother," Octavia told her. Transferring Ferren back to her shoulder, she handed back the book. "Thank you for your help."

Haf resignedly took the aged tome. "If you won't change your minds, let me see if I have something that will help you." Placing the book back on its shelf, she rummaged through an array of bottles. "Aha! This might work; sprinkle it over yourselves when you enter the marsh to disguise your scent and conceal yourselves. It will give you time to get near without alerting the wyvern to your presence. But be aware that it will not last long."

Beatrice took the bottle and placed it in her tunic pocket. After they had taken their leave of Haf, who watched them worriedly from her doorstep, the girls decided to go and find Evony.

Briar and Sorrel took them to the training yard, where they watched the warriors train from an observation balcony above. Evony was guiding a crystal arrow into her bow when she saw the girls on the balcony.

"Please come and join me!" she shouted up.

The girls made their way down the balcony's staircase into the circular yard, where various creatures and fairies were partaking in combat training. All wore the rainbow tabards or bands of the queen's guard.

Evony passed her gaze over the girls. After a moment's deliberation, she settled upon Felicity.

"Would you like to have a try?" Evony held out the bow, and Felicity looked at the golden curve. Octavia saw something stir in her sister's eyes and knew that Felicity was intrigued.

"Go on, Fliss," she encouraged.

Felicity grasped the bow with a nervous smile and said, "All right."

Evony took her to one side and gave her a few instructions. Felicity licked her lips nervously but inhaled slowly, holding her breath as Evony had said, and let loose the arrow, which missed the target. Felicity let out a self-deprecating laugh.

"Good. Again," Evony commanded, re-nocking the arrow. Octavia, Martha and Beatrice took a seat on a wooden bench and watched as the princess instructed Felicity for the next half-hour, each time the arrow getting nearer to the target. Various creatures and fairies stopped to observe, intrigued by the human girl and her mounting skill.

Finally, the girls held their breath as Felicity released another arrow. It shot through the air, the sunlight refracting through the crystal shaft as it hit its mark dead centre. Felicity let out a jubilant whoop, which made Octavia start in surprise; it felt like she was seeing her sister, the real her, for the first time.

But then again it had been there all along; during the lonely days spent missing Mum and Dad, Felicity had always been a constant, comforting presence. Always strong and focused while Octavia struggled. Now it was time for Felicity to have her moment to shine, and Octavia felt nothing but awe for her clever older sister.

"I got it that time!" Felicity said to Evony with a smile which lit up her face.

"I do believe you are a natural," Evony remarked with an answering smile, retrieving the arrow.

The assembled crowd of warriors broke into a smattering of applause, and, blushing, Felicity gave a quirky little bow. Ferren squeaked in celebration from Octavia's pocket.

"Well done, Fliss," Octavia said, pride colouring her voice. Felicity turned her soft green eyes on Octavia, and a shared moment of understanding passed between the sisters.

"That's enough training for now," said Evony. "I suggest a light meal and some rest. We have an arduous journey ahead of us."

Back in the Amethyst room, the girls sat around a crystal table and ate sweet bread and strawberries.

"I could get used to this," Beatrice mumbled through a mouthful of berries, which were being rolled over to her by a round Ferren.

"I want this quest over with so we can go back home," Martha answered, frowning at her sister, who had berry stains on her fingertips.

Octavia watched Felicity, who was daydreaming, which was most out of character. "Are you all right, Fliss?" she asked.

Felicity jumped. "Oh, yes. I was thinking about Mum and how she must be feeling."

Octavia suppressed a brief pang of guilt. "We need to get the flower, and everything will be better." She took her sister's hand and gave it a reassuring squeeze.

"I know, but it isn't going to be that easy, Tavi," Felicity said sensibly, and she got up to pace in a way reminiscent of their mother.

A knock at the door had all four girls turning in anticipation. Briar stood in the doorway. "It's time," she told them solemnly.

Sorrel entered the room and handed out leather bags and pearly water bottles to each of the girls. "Your supplies are in there."

Octavia had the tingling in her fingers again, but the mood was sombre as the girls followed the two forest fairies out into the courtyard, where the whole castle court had congregated. The queen stood on a raised dais and spoke to the girls.

"Bloom daughters, I have gifts for you that will assist you in your quest. Key Keeper, you will need this dagger and transportation box. Use the dagger to cut the Arianthe flower's stem when you find it and place it inside the box. I have enchanted it to transport the flower to your Fairy Door. Your mother will know what to do with it." Octavia accepted the short crystal dagger, decorated with a rainbow of jewels along its hilt. The glass box was shaped like a miniature treasure chest.

"To you, Guardian, I give bow and arrows. You will help protect and guard your sister. Princess Evony has told me of your natural affinity with archery; she will be your mentor."

Felicity looked stunned as she took the golden bow and rainbow-coloured quiver, which was full of crystal arrows.

"Secret Keepers, I give to you a compass to guide you to the North" – a glass compass was passed to Martha – "and revealing dust which will clear you a path through the marshes." Queen Rhosyn placed a glass bottle full of shimmering dust in Beatrice's hands.

"Thank you," the girls murmured to the queen, who inclined her head.

"And lastly, to my precious daughter, who has made me proud this day, I give one rainbow; it will transport you all here safely if needed. But use it wisely." The queen passed Evony a cloud-shaped hinged box. Evony curtsied low to her mother and placed the rainbow into her satchel.

"I wish you fairy blessings and safe passage. We will celebrate your return at the Late Summer Night Ball." She raised her hands, and a large rainbow appeared from her staff. "Step upon it; it will take you to Bloomsville Village."

The four girls took one last look around the fairy court. Led by Aurus, his magnificent golden coat gleaming in the sunlight, they stepped onto the rainbow, Evony following.

Wind rushed past Octavia's ears, and her stomach swooped as if she was on a slide; she closed her eyes tightly against the sensations. Ferren buried her head into the crook of Octavia's neck and squeaked softly as Octavia held her safely. After a few seconds, Octavia's feet touched solid ground and she slowly opened her eyes to find that they had arrived in a village square. Fairies and woodland creatures bustled about carrying baskets of flowers, bread and fruit.

"Princess Evony!" A squat fairy with long white hair hurried over, his moth-like wings fluttering furiously in his haste. "What brings you to Bloomsville?" he enquired.

"Good afternoon, Finnian. We are on a quest to the North: the Bloom girls here need to procure an Arianthe flower," Evony told him.

Finnian eyed the girls with interest. "Brave human girls," he murmured. "How can we be of assistance?"

"We require five of your best unicorns, if you would be so kind," Evony said. "We will pay you, of course," she added, holding up a leather bag full of clinking coins.

As Finnian and Evony stepped to one side to negotiate a price, the girls looked at each with excitement. Unicorns!

Evony rejoined the group and noted the girls' excitement. "You do ride?" she enquired. They all nodded mutely in anticipation, though Octavia frowned in confusion,

"But do you not fly everywhere?" she blurted out, then flushed as Felicity threw her a look that told Octavia she had spoken without thinking again.

Evony let out a musical laugh. "We can fly, of course,

but certainly not for long distances. Some wings are stronger than others, but our usual mode of transportation is by unicorn for long distances or bubble for short travels; or on rare occasions my mother will send us by rainbow, as you have just experienced."

Octavia studied Evony's wings with interest. Suddenly Aurus nodded his great head to the girls' left, and they watched in rising wonder as Finnian walked ahead of a fairy who was leading five of the most breathtaking creatures they had ever seen. Unlike the unicorns in Octavia's books, these were not pure white; their white coats were overlaid with a pattern of various blooming flowers and vines, their manes and tails perfectly matching the colour of the flowers. Each had a twisted rainbow horn on top of its head. Glittering rainbows sparked from their hooves where they struck the ground.

"Ohhhh!" breathed Octavia, and with rounded eyes the girls walked toward them.

"These are special Bloomsville unicorns," Evony explained. "They have an affinity with the realm."

Octavia gazed at the bright, flowery coats. "They're so colourful!"

"That is because Fairy Land is thriving and happy, of course," Finnian told Octavia proudly.

Octavia pondered this, but all thought left her mind as she locked eyes with the unicorn with yellow blooms. It whinnied in greeting.

"This is Xanthe," said Finnian. "She has chosen you!

Put your hand out – don't be afraid."

Octavia swallowed and slowly walked toward the yellow unicorn, her hand shaking with excitement as she placed it upon the creature's nose. Xanthe blew softly. They gazed at each other and Octavia's heart rate settled, a stillness coming over her.

Felicity paired up with Emeraude, a soft-eyed, green-patterned unicorn mare, and Martha with Linnea, a small unicorn patterned with pink flowers. The largest of the unicorns, a stallion with bold blue blooms, pawed at the air before sinking into a deep bow before Beatrice.

"You are honoured, Miss; Caeruleus has chosen you," Finnian said, chuckling.

Beatrice, who looked terrified at the very thought of riding him, visibly trembled as she walked toward Caeruleus, but after one look into his twinkling eyes, her face relaxed into a grin and she patted his great head. Meanwhile, Evony greeted her purple-hued unicorn, Ione, warmly.

As the girls mounted their unicorns, a thunder of hooves and shouts heralded the arrival of a riding party. The lead fairy, a young man with flowing, deep purple hair, dismounted as the unicorn was still running and flew directly to Finnian on powerful jewel-coloured wings. Octavia immediately saw what Evony had meant about some fairies' wings being stronger than others; this fairy's wings beat in the air like a large bird's. He did a double-take as he saw Evony and the girls.

Sinking into a low bow mid-flight, he enquired, "Princess, what are you doing in Bloomsville?"

He flushed as Evony raised one imperious eyebrow.

"We are on royal business, Soren," she said, a touch of her mother in her tone.

"Forgive me, but I must speak to the village elders immediately," he replied apologetically as he landed. Turning to Finnian, he said, "Father, the flower fields have been decimated."

Finnian gasped. "Wait here – I will gather the others!" He flew off to the largest building in the square.

Evony grasped Soren's strong arm. "What do you mean?" she asked him urgently.

"We went to collect more flowers for the Late Summer ceremony, but when we arrived, we found that the whole area has been burned and the soil churned up – there is not a blossom left," Soren told her.

"This is Nesrin's doing!" Evony seethed with anger. "Soren, please send a messenger to the castle and let my mother know. We have to go now, girls – there is not a moment to lose!" she continued, flying up to sit on Ione's back.

"Ev— Princess, where are you going? If this is indeed Nesrin's doing, it is not safe for you, nor them." Soren nodded to the girls.

"Do as I command. The queen needs to know about this. These girls have a curse to break." Evony met Soren's eyes, and he reluctantly nodded.

Wheeling her unicorn around, Evony addressed the girls. "Now you are paired with your steeds, think about what you want them to do and they will do it." At a neigh from Linnea, she smiled and added, "As long as it's safe, of course."

Octavia looked around at her sister and cousins and saw similar looks of concentration on their faces. Closing her eyes, she could detect a faint trace of glowing yellow in her mind. She latched on to it and thought, *Go*. Immediately, Xanthe trotted forward, falling in with the other unicorns.

Octavia turned her head, watching Soren with interest as they moved away. He waited until they left the village, indecision written across his handsome features. Finally, he turned to meet his father, who was coming back with a group of older fairies, and Octavia faced forward and thought of what was to come next.

Eight

Wattle

OCTAVIA ENJOYED THE COOL STILLNESS OF THE WOODS as they followed a well-worn path through the trees. She took a moment to observe her sister and cousins, who were riding the unicorns confidently. Beatrice especially was glowing with happiness; she kept looking down at the blue-patterned unicorn in awe.

Ferren squeaked from Octavia's tunic's top pocket, "I've never ridden on a unicorn before."

Octavia gave her a conspiratorial wink and giggled before saying, "Me neither!"

After a little while, Evony led them out of the woods. "Martha, it is time to get out your compass. Across this brook is the Flower Fields and beyond that is the Middling Grounds, which is neither my mother's nor Nesrin's domain. The Flower Fields are as far as I have travelled," she said, dismounting Ione.

The girls followed suit and led their unicorns to the glittering stream to drink. Evony gestured for the girls to fill up their water bottles. "It is safe," she assured them at their hesitation.

They held their bottles in the water, Octavia immediately thinking of Otto as she caught sight of her reflection.

"My father used to bring me to this brook, but would never take me past the Flower Fields – he said it wasn't safe for a princess," Evony said, interrupting Octavia's thoughts.

"Ours is over-protective too," Octavia said in sympathy and with a touch of pride. "Where *is* your father?" she asked. "We never met him at the castle." She regretted it instantly as Evony's face fell.

The princess paused, then opened her mouth, but a shout hailed them from across the brook. Evony looked apologetically at Octavia and flew towards a small bridge where another fairy waited.

Octavia followed Evony with her eyes and looked beyond her. She gasped at the sight of enormous fields, totally scorched and ruined.

"What could have done it?" she asked.

Aurus stepped back from the brook, water droplets running down his shaggy coat. "Nesrin favours wyverns," he intoned, "but it is so rare for them to come this far

south."

Evony flew back to the group, frowning. "No, this does not look like the work of a wyvern," she mused, taking a seat on a fallen log. "Maybe she has a new weapon. Fern is trying to salvage what she can, but I fear it is a hopeless task," she added, nodding toward the fairy who was walking back to the field. She looked at Martha. "The compass?"

Martha took out the compass and held it out to Evony, who shook her head. "No; it will only work for you."

Martha started and looked at the compass resting in her palm, surprised to find that, unlike a regular compass, there were no letters printed on it. She held it tightly and murmured, "Where's North?"

Instantly, the arrow pointed left.

"Oh!" she said in surprise.

Aurus nodded. "Well done." Martha flushed with pleasure at the praise from the solemn stag.

Octavia was itching to get going again. She hastily shared a honey cake with Ferren and passed one to Xanthe, who had bumped Octavia's shoulder with her head in a silent request.

"Time to go," Evony finally announced, to Octavia's relief.

They passed through the Flower Fields in single file, Evony at the front and Aurus bringing up the rear. That left the girls to focus on the devastation around them. Not a flower remained in the ground; the soil was charred and had deep troughs raked through it. Small sorting huts dotted around the edge of the field were burnt to their foundations. A ripple of unease skated down Octavia's back at the first sight of what Nesrin was capable of, but she shrugged it off; anything worth fighting for always came with its own risks.

Hoofbeats echoed along the road behind them, which had Aurus turning in one fluid movement, head and antlers braced downwards.

A voice rang out. "It is I – Soren."

Evony sighed audibly and put away her bow. "What are you doing here?" she called.

Soren joined them, sitting astride a large unicorn adorned with flame-coloured flowers. Its ruby mane sparkled in the late afternoon sun.

"I am here to assist you with your quest; the queen has agreed," he added with a sideways look at Evony, who frowned. She let out a frustrated breath and threw up her hands.

"Very well. Please ride between Felicity and Beatrice." She pointed to the middle, introduced the girls to Soren, and recapped the details of their quest for him.

"The Arianthe flower?" he asked, disbelieving. "That's ridiculous! I've heard they hatch from wyvern's eggs!" he blustered.

"We know," Evony said wryly. "Still want to come along?"

Soren stiffened, but didn't reply. He silently slotted

his unicorn between Emeraude and Caeruleus. Octavia exchanged glances with Felicity; the air was suddenly thick with tension. Evony started Ione walking and they all followed, a quiet procession through the ruins of the flower fields.

Xanthe started to tremble beneath Octavia. Perplexed, she looked down and gasped. Xanthe's bright, patterned flanks were dimming, the colours turning from vibrant to pastel before her eyes. Octavia heard sounds of dismay from the other girls; their unicorns too were fading.

"Princess, look at Ember!" Soren shouted. Evony, brought out of her thoughts, wheeled around to stare at Soren's unicorn. The flaming flowers licking up his legs were winking out as if being doused by buckets of water. "Something is wrong," Soren said, leaping off Ember to stand at his nose. Ember braced his large head on Soren's shoulder weakly.

"Why are their flowers fading?" Beatrice asked nervously. Soren grimaced and met Evony's eyes; a knowing look passed between them.

"I could tell you," a whiny voice remarked. The group turned as one. On the threshold between the Flower Fields and the Middling Grounds' woods stood a scruffy weasel, a dirty, ripped tabard hanging limply from one shoulder.

"Your Highness, stand back," Aurus commanded, cantering to stand in front of Evony and the girls.

"I mean you no harm, Princess, nor to your human friends," the weasel simpered, tiny paws outstretched.

Ferren popped her head out of Octavia's pocket and squeaked at the sight of the weasel, who almost imperceptibly licked his lips as his eyes landed on the tiny mouse. She quickly retreated into the depths of the pocket.

"Do not listen to him! I recognise the tabard of Queen Nesrin's guard." Aurus snorted, pawing the ground. The unicorns huddled together feebly, and Soren watched them, worriedly running a hand over Ember's flanks.

"I have been banished; my loyalties lie with Nesrin no longer!" the weasel protested. "See? My tabard has been ripped as part of my banishment." He held up what had obviously once been a smart black tabard, emblazoned with silver stars.

Evony stepped out from behind Aurus. "What is your name, and what caused your banishment?" she demanded.

"I am Wattle, your highness." The weasel gave a crooked bow. "I decided I no longer had a taste for hurting innocents. I refused to help ruin the Flower Fields, something Nesrin did not look favourably upon." He hung his head. "She banished me to the Middling Grounds."

Evony looked thoughtful. "He could be a useful source of information," she said.

Aurus and Soren exchanged looks. "I don't like this; it could be a trap," Soren vetoed.

"*I* will decide what to do with him," Evony replied. "Tell me, weasel, what caused the destruction of the

Flower Fields? If you assist Queen Rhosyn in bringing the perpetrators to justice, she may look favourably upon you."

Wattle rubbed his paws overs his whiskers. "May I have some food and water first, please? It has been hours since I ate and drank," he said slyly.

Evony raised an eyebrow and made to offer her water bottle, but Soren beat her to it and thrust his upon the weasel, who took it greedily. After he had drunk his fill and eaten three honey cakes, he sat on a nearby tree stump and belched. Octavia had to stifle a giggle.

Aurus looked down his golden snout and pawed the ground. "Sneaky weasel, answer the princess' question."

"Nesrin has struck a bargain with the fire imps. In return for razing the Flower Fields, she will give them Rhosyn's Woods," the weasel announced, gratified at the gasps that came from Evony, Soren and Aurus.

"How dare she! They are not Nesrin's to gift," Evony expostulated, her eyes sparking with outrage.

"If Nesrin's plan works, it soon will be," Wattle replied, ending on a squeak as he found himself hoisted in the air, dangling by the remnants of his tattered tabard on Aurus' gigantic antlers.

"What plan?" Aurus growled, great puffs of breath making the little weasel swing.

"Sh-she is betting on the Bloom girl failing her quest to save her brother and her mother, the current Key Keeper, losing all hope. If she stops believing in us,

Fairy Land will weaken, which in turn will weaken Queen Rhosyn's magic. The Key Keepers do not just look after the key to the door to our realm; they are also the last true believers," Wattle rambled. "Please put me down! I feel sick," he moaned.

"That's all those honey cakes you ate, you greedy little weasel!" Aurus told him, placing him roughly back on the tree stump.

Octavia looked at Felicity and saw the shock she was feeling mirrored on her sister's face.

"It looks like it has already started." Wattle nodded at the solemn unicorns, the colours on their blooming flanks wilted and pale.

Soren nodded. "I have never seen this happen before, but my father has always warned me that if the unicorns start to fade then there is something seriously wrong with the realm. I didn't realise how quickly and badly it would affect the unicorns."

Octavia spoke up. "But Mum would never give up! She is the strongest person I know!"

"Maybe the fact that she has now lost all three of her children to Fairy Land has broken her," Felicity said sadly.

With a swoop in her stomach, guilt settled over Octavia like a heavy cloud – a feeling she couldn't suppress this time.

Martha started to cry. "I want to go home; I've had enough of this place!" she sobbed. Beatrice dismounted and walked to her sister's side; she gripped her hand

tightly.

"We can do this, Matty! We've come this far," she consoled her. Martha continued to cry quietly.

Evony looked thunderstruck. "I of course knew the unicorn's blooms were connected to the health of the realm, but why didn't my mother ever tell me that the future of our land depended on a family of humans believing in us?"

"I'm sure the queen had her reasons," Wattle said ingratiatingly, and tried for an encouraging smile, which looked more like a grimace to Octavia.

Evony stared at him. "You will come with us. If you try to double-cross us in any way, I will let Aurus deal with you."

Wattle gulped visibly as he looked at Aurus, who pulled back his lips in a parody of a menacing grin. Soren scowled, but mounted Ember with care. The unicorns walked more slowly as they entered the Middling Grounds' woods, adjusting to their weaker state. Evony placed an arrow in her bow as they passed underneath a thick canopy of leaves, her eyes scanning the area.

Aurus walked up besides Octavia and gestured ahead with his antlers. "Be on your guard; the Middling Grounds are home to fairy folk and creatures that live on the fringes of society – neither of Queen Rhosyn's or Nesrin's court. Although Nesrin has been known to recruit some of the Middling Market's more... *questionable* characters from time to time," he explained quietly, his eyes alert.

Martha gulped audibly and Beatrice, who was riding next to her, reached over and patted her arm.

They exited the woods and passed through a shabby village where crooked huts and tumbledown shacks lined the street. Shutters slammed, and Octavia caught glimpses of winged folk and furry creatures sliding out of sight.

Keeping to the left, as shown by Martha's compass, they left the village and carried on; the ground sloped downward into a rocky ravine, cliffs towering on either side of them. Wattle whimpered and hopped in pain as his small feet were caught by jagged stones. Aurus sneered and lifted the weasel up, setting him on his back in disgust. Wattle gripped tightly to the golden fur, his eyes widening in terror as he looked at the distant ground below.

They passed through the ravine with no incident, and Soren and Aurus breathed more easily as they came to a waterfall surrounded by a small copse of trees.

"We will camp here for the night," Evony announced, disembarking from Ione and leading her to the pool at the bottom of the waterfall to drink. The unicorn lapped thirstily before lying down in the shade of a small tree.

Dusk was falling; the sky was painted in the lilacs, blues and pinks of sunset, but here in Fairy Land it glittered with a thousand fireflies as well as they danced together, flocking like sparrows.

Soren took over care of the unicorns as Octavia, Felicity, Martha and Beatrice sat together at the pool's edge. Fortifying themselves with the refreshing water, they watched the sunset, Martha drawing a map of their journey with a piece of black crystal and a scrap of parchment from Evony's satchel.

Octavia was aware of Evony, Soren and Aurus deep in discussion; the worried tones were not lost on her. Wattle strained to hear what was being said, whilst nonchalantly rummaging through the supplies bag for yet more honey cakes.

"We need to ration our supplies; we did not bring a food fairy with us," Aurus remarked sarcastically, looking over at the weasel. Wattle dropped the honey cake as if it had grown warm between his paws. He guiltily slunk over to the pool near the girls.

Martha looked at the little weasel in disgust as he aimed a toothy grin at her. "What a pretty trinket," he said in an oily manner, looking at the compass by her feet.

She immediately picked it up and placed it inside her supply bag. "It's a gift from the queen," she told him dismissively.

"Fortunate girl, favoured by the queen. I, too, was a favourite of my queen; alas, no more," he remarked sadly, shaking his whiskery head.

Evony frowned as she saw Wattle talking to the girls. Walking over, she told them, "You should get some sleep; we have the most dangerous part of our travels tomorrow." Pointing at Wattle, she added, "You will sleep next to Aurus. I am on first watch."

Wattle gave a gulp and slunk over next to Aurus, where he curled up on a bed of moss and closed his eyes. Aurus eyed him for a moment before lying down facing the weasel.

The girls rolled out their blankets and snuggled close together. Octavia lay on her back, staring up at the indigo sky, where the first stars where beginning to twinkle.

Something woke Octavia. She took a second to steady her breathing before she rolled over. Ferren had been whispering her name softly into her ear; as Octavia turned her eyes upon her, the little mouse gestured. Wattle was standing next to her, his quick paws going through her satchel. She watched him silently as he took out the transportation box and examined it. He opened it but, finding it empty, returned it to the bag. He glanced around furtively, jumping violently as he saw Octavia looking at him.

"Oh, Key Keeper, you are awake!" he stalled, stepping back from the bag. "I was, um, looking for more honey cakes," he announced, trying for a charming smile.

Octavia narrowed her eyes. "Really?" she asked, disbelieving. The was a rustle from the nearby bush. Wattle scampered back to his mossy bed and tightly closed his eyes. Soren appeared from behind the bush, eyes scanning the darkness. Looking satisfied that nothing was amiss, he resumed his post.

Feeling too sleepy to enlighten him, Octavia decided to talk to Evony in the morning about Wattle. Rolling over, she readily succumbed to sleep once more.

Nine

The Misty North

THE SUN WARMED OCTAVIA'S FACE and awakened her slowly; busy sounds around the campsite brought her fully awake and she sat up.

"Good morning." Evony's soft voice came from behind her. "Come, join us."

Octavia turned around to see her sister, cousins, Evony, Soren and Aurus seated around a small fairy fire hovering above the ground, its flames burning with rainbow hues. Wattle didn't meet her eyes as she passed him and took a seat next to Felicity. Evony passed her a cup of steaming peppermint tea, its aroma blowing away the last vestiges of sleepiness.

"What is the plan for today?" Octavia asked Evony, reaching for a slice of bread and a handful of juicy berries

to share with Ferren.

"I estimate we should be at Misty Marsh soon; we will need to be careful as we enter the area – it is deeply into Nesrin's kingdom, so ambush is most likely. Felicity, I will give you another archery lesson whilst the others pack up the camp," Evony said, standing. She had braided her long teal hair, twisting it around her head like a crown. She stretched out her strong wings, soaking up the sun's rays. Octavia caught Soren staring and hid a smile behind her cup.

Soren gave himself a shake and quickly stood to help pack up and tend to the unicorns, who had faded even more overnight, as Evony and Felicity headed further away from the group to practice.

"You, weasel, gather some water." Aurus nudged the water bottles in Wattle's direction. Wattle scowled and slunk off, tiny arms full of bottles almost as big as him.

"My compass – my compass is gone!" Martha cried suddenly, tipping her bag upside down and shaking everything out. Remembering Wattle's night-time wanderings, Octavia's eyes immediately went to the weasel, whose back stiffened as he finished capping the water bottles.

Beatrice rushed to help Martha look for the compass, who was starting to panic. Octavia felt a sudden sympathy for her eldest cousin; she had been struggling the most with being away from home and was clearly terrified at the thought of being stuck in Fairy Land. Her thoughts turned back to Wattle as he staggered back to the campsite with the bottles of water.

"I will get the princess," Aurus said solemnly.

Wattle shuffled over to his bed of moss and sat, looking twitchy.

"*You* haven't seen the compass, have you?" Octavia asked him. Yes, she wasn't imagining it – he looked decidedly guilty.

Evony, Felicity and Aurus returned to the clearing, and Evony frowned as she watched the weasel's reaction. He wouldn't meet anyone's eyes, and he wrung his little paws in agitation. Aurus gave a low grunt and stalked toward Wattle, who cowered in fright. As the stag towered over Wattle, words burst out, tumbling over each other in terror.

"I – I thought I could sell it at the Middling Market. I'm without coin now that I have been banished!" He retrieved the compass from the depths of the moss and held it out. With a cry of relief, Martha rushed over to grab it and clutched it tightly to her chest.

Evony pulled out a long wand that looked like a miniature version of her mother's staff. Wattle shrank back, but instead of pointing it at him she waved it delicately in the air to create a golden chain which attached itself to the compass.

"It will be safer on you." She lowered the chain over Martha's neck and watched as Martha tucked it beneath her tunic. Wattle looked dismayed as the compass disappeared from his view.

Soren pulled Evony aside. "That weasel is not to be trusted," he hissed in a loud whisper. Aurus snorted in agreement.

"I caught him going through my bag last night," Octavia weighed in with a wary look at the weasel, who was straining to hear their conversation.

Evony turned her back on Wattle. "I agree we cannot trust him, but I think it prudent to keep him close," she whispered back. Looking at the sun, which was climbing higher in the sky, she said more loudly, "Time to go."

The party was once again led by Evony, with Martha following, giving instructions from the compass. They carried on over rocky ground until they entered a dark forest; mist hung low over the forest floor, and purple-spotted toadstools sprouted from the damp ground.

The compass in Martha's trembling hand hadn't moved since they entered the forest; they were truly in the north now. They pressed on, the trees growing closer together and obscuring the winding track.

The unicorns stopped and refused to go any deeper, the blooms on their coats now so faded it was hard to see them. Soren exchanged a worried look with Evony. Gesturing with her head, she led Ione over to a small clearing off the track, the others following.

"What shall we do?" Soren asked, rubbing a comforting hand over Ember's trembling back.

Evony opened her mouth to reply, but a dazed look

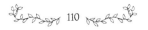

came over her as a rainbow shot through the wood, solidifying into a piece of parchment in her hand. The girls watched in bewilderment, Evony's face paling as she read the note. She looked at Octavia and Felicity in concern.

"Your mother is at Castle Enfys. The Key Keeper tried to use some of the transportation dust my mother bestowed upon your family to send any boy babies here," Evony told them worriedly.

Felicity gasped. "Is she all right?"

"I am afraid she is gravely hurt; the dust is not intended for human adults. Hevva is working to save her."

"We must turn back – we must go to her!"

Evony gave Felicity a look of sympathy, but shook her head. "No, it is imperative now more than ever that we endeavour forth. We have one chance to get the flower and to end this!"

Felicity put a shaky hand on Octavia's arm. "Tavi?" she murmured tremulously.

Octavia had been staring at the edge of the forest where the mist shrouded the landscape. An angry determination had befallen her.

"We go on. We finish what we set out to do. Mum is in the best possible care. We will serve no purpose by turning back now," she told her sister. Ferren crawled out from Octavia's tunic pocket and sat upon her shoulder, where she patted Octavia's cheek in comfort.

"The unicorns cannot go on," Soren reminded them in a sombre voice. The blooms had faded until they were almost imperceptible to the eye.

Evony's gaze turned thoughtful. "Aurus, you will stay here with the unicorns," she said.

He shook his great head. "I will not let you go on alone, Princess; I am sworn to protect you and the girls."

Evony expanded her wings and looked at him. "I *need* you to stay with the unicorns. We will use Haf's concealment dust to make our way through the marsh and retrieve the flower. Afterwards we will come straight back and use the rainbow to transport ourselves out of here – I promise. I will not take any unnecessary risks. Please, Aurus; the unicorns cannot go another step." Her tone brooked no argument.

Aurus breathed heavily and pawed the ground. He looked at the six unicorns in their pale state and finally nodded. "I will stay with them."

Wattle looked relieved as Aurus agreed to stay behind, and smirked smugly.

Aurus glared down at the weasel. "If you so much as think about stealing from or betraying any one of them, I will find you," he promised.

Wattle's smirk vanished as if it had been erased.

The girls took their leave of their unicorn friends sadly. Octavia hoped they would see them in all their blooming glory again soon; they just had to get the flower, and get Mum believing once more. *Easy*, she thought wryly, stroking Ferren absentmindedly. The little mouse had taken to hiding in her tunic pocket, out of sight of

Wattle.

They left Aurus and the six silent unicorns in the clearing, and Evony addressed the remaining group. "Here is the plan. I will lead us to the edge of Misty Marsh; girls, you follow, with Soren and Wattle bringing up the rear. At the edge of the marsh we will use Haf's dust to conceal ourselves. Beatrice, you will walk with me, using the dust my mother gave you to clear a safe path through the marsh." She looked around questioningly; the rest nodded their agreement.

The trees had thinned out and the ground began to squelch underfoot, the mist clinging to their cloaks as they headed into the marsh.

"Beatrice, the dust," Evony requested.

Beatrice put her hand into her satchel and retrieved the two bottles. She stared down at the similar bottles, confusion etched across her face. Octavia watched her cousin seemingly come to a decision and hand the slightly larger one to Evony, who started to sprinkle it over everyone.

They plunged on through the marsh. Evony used her wand to light the way as Beatrice sprinkled dust in front of them, but still the mist remained, obscuring their vision.

"I don't understand! Why is it not working?" Evony whispered, sidestepping a large electric-green toadstool that glowed through the gloom.

Beatrice gulped nervously as the mist started to envelop them, cutting them off from each other. Soren kept a tight grip of Wattle's tabard, as if fearing the weasel would sneak off.

A crack split the air and sudden static lifted the girls' hair. Evony let out a shout and grabbed her bow. A laughing cackle surrounded the group; they spun around, looking for the source.

"Oh dear! Did somebody mix up their fairy dusts?" A sinuous voice asked with a laugh. "They can't see me, but I can see them, oh yes."

Octavia's heart was in her throat. She grasped in the mist and felt a hand. "Fliss, is that you?" she whispered.

The hand grasped back tightly. They moved closer together; the swirling mist parted briefly, and in the milky light Felicity's pale face was revealed.

A silver beam shot from Octavia's left and lit up a circle around her feet; it pulsed, growing until it illuminated the ghost-like faces of the other girls, Evony, and Soren, who was clutching his wrist.

"That dratted weasel bit me," he groaned.

"Princess Evony, welcome to my marsh. I am most honoured. Your dear mother would not have come," a voice sneered. Gliding over the boggy ground came Nesrin, her face twisted into an evil smile, her raven flying behind her like a black shadow. The silver light was coming from her glowing staff.

The girls huddled together as Evony followed Nesrin's progress with her bow and arrow. Soren glared at Wattle who stood, bowing reverently before his queen.

"Traitorous creature," Soren hissed.

Nesrin looked at Soren. "On the contrary, this is my most loyal guard. He would do anything for his queen." She gestured for Wattle to straighten, then frowned. "Although he failed to stop you getting this far…"

Wattle twisted his paws nervously. "My queen, I thought you would wish to deal with them yourselves; I know how much pleasure you will gain in seeing them fail," he simpered.

Nesrin furrowed her brow further. "That is true. However, Taran will deal with you later," she told the now trembling weasel as he looked at the raven, whose cruel beak curved ruthlessly.

On a sudden move, Nesrin aimed her staff at Evony. The beam of light fractured the crystal arrow into a thousand pieces. Evony dropped her bow and yelped. Blood glistened on her fingertips where the crystal shards had cut her. Soren went to draw his short sword, but stopped as Nesrin aimed her staff at him.

"Enough of this nonsense! I am tired of playing hide-and-seek with you!" she screeched.

She floated over to the girls and aimed her laser-like gaze upon Beatrice, who hid behind Martha. Octavia made to step toward her, but paused as Nesrin shot a dismissive glance her way before turning back to Beatrice.

"Poor child, always in your sister's shadow. Trying to be important… but look at what you've done." She glanced at the rest of the group. "You let my trusting niece sprinkle you all in revealing dust! You all glowed like fireflies walking through my marsh."

Nesrin gave a harsh laugh, but Beatrice moaned in horror as the dark fairy's words sank in.

"Don't fret, my dear, you would do well in my court; you would be treated like a princess. I would mould you in my image and make you my heir." Nesrin's voice had taken on a mesmerising tone as she looked deep into Beatrice's eyes.

"No! She will not go with you!" Martha found her voice, shaking in her terror. She put her arms around her sister and held her close.

"No? I shall make her come whilst you brave souls deal with *this!*" Nesrin raised her arms, her black wings fully extending as she struck the ground with her staff. Silver lightning bolts zigzagged across the floor and a screech echoed around the marsh. A huge shadow flew overhead, circling.

Nesrin smiled coldly as she grabbed hold of Beatrice, stepped onto her black cloud – Wattle nimbly following – and vanished. Taran's echoing caws fading away as they disappeared.

"Noooo!" Martha wailed, and she turned angrily on Octavia. "This is all your fault! You and your desperate need for adventure. I never wanted to come here in the first place, and look what has happened now – Bea is gone!"

Octavia felt the blood drain from her face as Martha's

words cut her deeply. Horrified at this turn of events, she stepped forward to try to hug Martha, who shrugged her off. As Martha did so, her foot came down heavily on a cluster of the green toadstools. A puff of vile-smelling green liquid shot up and hit her square in the face. She instantly buckled and fell slowly toward the spongy ground. Soren leapt forward to catch her, and a burst of the foul liquid covered him too.

Evony waved her wand in a swift pattern, which stopped their fall to the ground. They hovered like pale ghosts in the mist. Evony flicked her wand, and the two figures floated to her side; she gently lowered them to a large piece of bark.

Octavia and Felicity looked at each other in shock and fell to their knees beside the unconscious pair, Octavia clutching Martha's hand desperately. Another screech, closer this time, split the air. Evony looked up apprehensively.

"We have a difficult choice to make. Your cousin and Soren have been hit by a slumbershroom. If they don't get the antidote soon there will be no waking them," she told the girls grimly. "We can leave and save them, but that will mean forgetting the flower – and not being able to save Otto, possibly your mother, and now Beatrice."

Octavia gazed pensively at Martha's still face, and guilt settled heavily upon her chest. Martha had been right; if Octavia hadn't pushed for them to all go through the Fairy Door, then Martha *and* Beatrice wouldn't be in this predicament. The need to save her cousins and all her family rose within her like a determined surge. It ran down her arms, causing her fingers to tingle with adrenaline. Slowly standing, her back straight and her head held high, she met Evony's curious gaze.

"What if we can do it all?" Octavia suggested with determination, "You and Aurus can use the rainbow and take Martha, Soren and the unicorns back to Castle Enfys. Felicity and I will go on and find the flower. I will send it back to Grandmother and Great-Aunt Clara; they can make Otto's cure. Then we can regroup and save Beatrice together."

Respect bloomed within Evony's eyes, but she shook her head. "No. It is too dangerous; I will go on. You can take the others back."

Octavia took a deep breath. "Princess Evony... I'm the one who has to finish it. I can feel it. It has to be me!"

Evony looked taken aback for a moment; then, finally, she nodded. "Very well, but after you have secured the flower, wait in the clearing. As soon as Martha and Soren are safe, I will ask my mother to send a rainbow back for you." She looked at the two bottles, which had fallen to the ground after Beatrice had been whisked away. "At least we now know which dust is which. There is enough for you two." She looked at Felicity, who was still staring at Martha in shock.

"Felicity, can you do this? Can you assist your sister? You will need to be calm and keep a steady hand; you will only get one shot at the wyvern."

Felicity jumped as Evony addressed her. "Ye... yes, I can do it," she stuttered, and then she took a deep breath.

Octavia watched a change come over her sister. A steely light shone in Felicity's eyes and she stood. Reaching for her bow, she took out a single crystal arrow, ready to face what was coming.

Ten

Come What May

OCTAVIA AND FELICITY WATCHED EVONY use her wand to float Martha and Soren in the direction of the clearing where Aurus waited. The princess turned back to give the girls one final nod before the mist closed around her like a curtain. The sisters were on their own now.

Octavia sprinkled the remains of the concealing dust over them. A long, drawn-out screech sounded from the girls' right. Keeping close together, Octavia and Felicity used the last of the revealing dust to find a safe path through the marsh, making sure to avoid any slumbershrooms.

A gloriously full moon came out from behind the clouds, lighting up the area like a beacon. Still shrouded

by the dust, the girls stood in its beam, hidden from the now-circling wyvern, whose form was revealed by the moonlight.

Felicity followed it with her arrow, but Octavia's gasp stopped her from taking the shot. On a mossy mound, surrounded by a nest fashioned from golden coins and crystals, was an opaque egg with purple veins running through it. As the Late Summer Moon's light hit the egg, it shattered; a lone purple flower rose from the remains, its spiky petals unfurling one by one.

Mesmerised, Octavia walked toward it, feeling in her satchel for her dagger. Ferren, who had retreated deep into Octavia's pocket, poked her head out to see. She suddenly gave a frightened yell. "Look out!"

The wyvern had turned its great, scaly head toward the girls, and furls of smoke snaked out of its snout.

"The dust must be wearing off! Run!" Felicity yelled. They both headed for the mound, sliding on the squelchy ground, and darted behind a twisted, blackened tree as the wyvern swooped low, flames coursing from its mouth. The creature gave a screech as it missed the girls.

Felicity nocked her arrow and turned in one swift move as the wyvern wheeled around, smoke pouring from its nostrils, gearing up for another onslaught. She closed her eyes briefly and breathed in slowly. Everything took on a dream-like quality; the pounding of Octavia's heart in her ears diminished all other sounds as she watched Felicity open her eyes and focus on one thing only: her target. Her sister let the arrow fly.

Octavia held her breath as she watched its flight; it seemed to arc in slow motion through the mist. With a colossal roar, the wyvern bucked and writhed in the air as the arrow found its mark and embedded itself deep in its chest. The smoke was extinguished from the creature's nostrils and the glow dimmed in its great eyes. On a final sigh and one last shudder, the wyvern disappeared in an explosion of glittery particles.

"You did it!" Octavia yelled, grabbing her sister and hugging her tightly.

Felicity let out a great sob and sank slowly to her knees, her pent-up emotions released like a flurry of arrows. She clutched at Octavia, who held her tightly as she cried.

She finally let out a heaving breath and lifted her watery eyes to Octavia's. Octavia looked back at her, feeling a mixture of sympathy and awe for her big sister.

"I'm sorry," Felicity sniffed, wiping her nose on the sleeve of her tunic.

"Don't be! I am so proud of you. We wouldn't have been able to finish the quest if it weren't for you," Octavia told her.

Felicity gave a shuddering breath and stood. She handed Octavia the dagger, which had dropped to the floor. "Then finish it," she told her, smiling.

They approached the mound together, hand in hand. Ferren ran ahead of them, squeaking in excitement.

Taking a deep breath, Octavia knelt in front of the flower, taking in the enormity of the situation. Reverently, she stroked the violet petals, which tinkled lightly at her touch. She gently took the dagger, and with one swipe cut the stem. Five purple, crystalline seeds exploded from the thick stalk; they flew in all directions. Four landed in the squelchy mud and disappeared, but the fifth landed in Felicity's outstretched hand. She looked down at it in surprise and then raised her eyes to Octavia, who grinned.

"I guess that one is yours!"

Felicity stared down at the glowing seed for a moment, before putting it into her bag.

Feeling that time was of the essence, Octavia swiftly opened the glass box, and with a look at her sister, placed the purple bloom inside. She closed the lid; the flower pulsed once with a bright purple light and was gone.

Octavia sagged with relief, and Felicity bent to rub her back soothingly. "It's not over yet, Tavi," she reminded her.

Octavia nodded.

Following the demise of the wyvern, the mist that covered the marsh had diminished greatly. The girls could make out trees, fallen logs and a pathway lit by glowing toadstools. At the end of the path stood a black mountain; atop it a silver castle jutted out, black banners waving in the wind.

The girls looked at each other again, and Octavia raised an eyebrow in question. Felicity shook her head.

"No. We did what we set out to do – we should go back and wait for the rainbow from Castle Enfys."

"But Nesrin's castle is right there! It wouldn't hurt to go and take a look to see what we're up against," Octavia wheedled, taking out her water bottle.

With a huff, Felicity sat on a log. "I can't make decisions when I'm hungry," she moaned, grabbing the last of the honey cakes and two apples from her bag. Sharing it out, the girls and Ferren munched silently.

"I knew you girls would be trouble," a watery voice croaked.

Felicity yelped as Lyffy crawled out from beneath the log. Octavia did a double-take before recognising the large toad they had encountered in Rhosyn's Woods when they had first arrived.

"How did *you* get here?" Ferren asked, astounded.

"I had business to attend to," he said disdainfully to the little mouse, whose whiskers twitched indignantly. "So, aside from felling wyverns, what is next on your agenda?" he enquired, hopping onto the log next to Octavia, his long tongue flicking out to latch onto a passing bug.

Octavia gazed at Nesrin's castle. "Do you know a way in there?" she asked, gesturing to the distant fortress.

"Castle Astra? Why would you want to go there?" he asked with an ill-disguised shudder.

"Nesrin has our cousin Beatrice – we need to rescue her!" Octavia began.

"No, we need to get back to Castle Enfys for

assistance," interrupted Felicity.

Lyffy looked from one to the other. "I do know one way in…" he mused. "But it is only fit for… a certain creature," he croaked delicately.

"Come on, Fliss, we've come this far. We can't leave Beatrice with Nesrin: we don't know what enchantments she will put on her."

Felicity sighed, and Octavia could sense her sister's desire to make sure Beatrice was safe overriding her naturally sensible nature. "Fine, but we just scope out the castle, then go back for reinforcements."

Octavia nodded fervently; wiping the honey-cake crumbs from her lap, she stood. "Lead on, Sir Lyffy," she ordered, tucking Ferren back in her pocket.

Lyffy puffed himself in an almost regal manner and croaked. He leapt from the log with surprising agility and hopped off along the pathway, the girls hastening to keep up with the toad. He kept to the edges of the path, gesturing to them periodically to duck behind the various bushes and twisted trees they passed.

The moon was fully overhead now. It was a magnificent sight: the Late Summer's Night Moon. It glowed, luminescent, a purple halo ringing its shining face. Octavia was full of a mix of relief at finally getting the flower and the prospect of meeting her brother soon and worry for Beatrice, Martha and her mother. She hoped they would not be sacrifices in the process of saving Otto.

Biting her lip, she nearly bumped into Felicity, who

had stopped at Lyffy's sudden gesture. He beckoned them behind a bush at the base of the mountain; they crouched next to him, silently gazing up the sheer cliffside. The sound of clanking caught their attention and they watched a silver gate in the castle walls slowly lift, letting out a series of small grey clouds, holding an assortment of creatures in black tabards. The clouds encircled the mountain, a guard standing sentry on each one, eyes scanning above and below.

"How are we going to get in?" Octavia whispered with a sideways glance at Felicity, who frowned.

"We don't," she hissed back. "Tavi, you promised."

"Shh!" Lyffy whispered. "This way." He crawled under the bush. "You won't be able to go back now without being seen. Nesrin must be worried about the repercussions of kidnapping your cousin, if she is posting extra guards," he told Felicity. They followed him through a gap in the bush, pushing their way out into a cave in the mountainside which was slippery with running water. Stalactites and stalagmites framed the entrance, black with veins of silver.

"In here – careful," Lyffy muttered, hopping onto a ledge. Felicity slipped on the shiny floor and grabbed onto Octavia to steady herself. A succession of rough steps had been hewn into the rock. Lyffy hopped up them, waiting for the girls to follow him. "This leads up to the," he cleared his throat, "ah, latrine chamber."

"Did you say latrine?" Felicity asked with a shudder.

Lyffy disguised a croaky chuckle. "I did say it was for creatures of a particular sort."

Felicity scowled at Octavia, but carried on up the steps.

When they stopped to catch their breath, Octavia noticed that the walls were becoming slimier, and a pungent smell wafted from an archway above their heads. They mounted the last few steps and crept through it, checking there was no one inside.

A large, fetid pool sat in the centre of the chamber; oily and black, it bubbled lazily. Covering their mouths and noses with their sleeves, the girls took shallow breaths. Ferren gave little squeaking coughs from within Octavia's pocket.

Lyffy gestured with a webbed hand to a ledge that ran the perimeter of the chamber; on the far side, above the pool, was a grate. "You need to go through there," he explained, pointing.

Felicity shuddered, but climbed onto the ledge after the toad, followed by Octavia, who swiftly checked Ferren was safely secured. They sidled their way gingerly around the ledge. Lyffy squeezed through the grate into a foul-smelling tunnel and looked back apologetically at the girls.

Felicity braced her knees on either side of the grate and, with Octavia's assistance, slid it upward. They froze at the loud creaking the grate gave, but after a few moments of silence they crawled through, pulling it securely down behind them. The tunnel sloped upwards, so they placed their feet on either side of the stinking trough that ran through it and shimmied their way up, their backs stooped, knees bent. They managed to get through the tunnel without stepping in anything, but the odour clung to their clothes like a cloak.

At the top there was a hole, big enough for buckets of filth to be tossed down. They waited until Lyffy had checked the coast was clear before pulling themselves through. Luckily, they were of delicate build and fitted easily.

Looking around, they found themselves in a large room filled with compartments and buckets – they were in a communal toilet block, Octavia thought with a grimace. Following Lyffy through the archway, they stopped in the corridor and listened; they could hear the distant clanging of the gate as the guards changed shifts.

They sidled down the corridor until they came to the end. Before they could look around the corner, a voice made them jump, causing Octavia to let out a surprised gasp.

"Well, well, what do we have here?" the familiar voice asked. Octavia looked down to see Wattle staring at her, his nose wrinkling in distaste.

"You!" she hissed, reaching down and gripping him by his tabard, which had been replaced with a pristine new one.

"Ugh, you'll get my uniform stinky," he moaned.

Twisting out of her grip, he ran four-legged along the corridor, shouting, "Guards! Intruders!"

"Oh no! What do we do?" Felicity panicked, looking around frantically.

"In here," a musical voice buzzed. Lyffy and the girls darted into the room opposite, where the voice had come from.

In the centre of the room, on a black onyx table, was a small cage in the shape of a beehive. A beautiful bee about the size of Ferren sat on a miniature throne inside it, a crown atop her fuzzy head, the gold fashioned to look like molten honey dripping from its points.

"Hide behind the zcreen! I will diztract them." Her lilting voice turned every s into a z.

Desperate, and with no time to lose, the girls made a quick decision to trust the bee. Darting behind the screen along with Lyffy, they held their breath as a guard came into the room.

"Where did they go – the two human girls?" he demanded.

"Human girlz? I have zeen no human girlzzz! How dare you dizturb me!" The queen bee flew angrily at the side of the cage, her stinger thrusting through a gap in the bars.

Eyeing the bee's stinger warily, the guard backed out of the room. "Sorry, Your Majesty," he muttered before fleeing.

"The coazt izzz clear," the queen bee buzzed softly.

Octavia and Felicity tentatively came out from behind the screen and looked down at the bee. "Thank you," Octavia said, nodding in respect.

"You are welcome. If you are intruderzzz at Queen Nezrin'zzz caztle, you are friendzzz of mine. I am Gwenyn, Queen of the Beezzz." She inclined her stripy head, her black eyes watching them with interest.

"Forgive me, Your Majesty, but how have you come to be locked up here?" Felicity asked, as Lyffy stood watch by the door.

Just then, Ferren popped her head out of Octavia's pocket with a squeak. "Queen Gwenyn!" she said in surprise.

"Ah, little Ferren, it is a pleazure to zee you again; you were juzt a little zqueakling the lazt time I zaw you." The bee smiled in genuine pleasure before answering Felicity. "Nezrin came to my palace; she uzed magical zmoke to zend my beezzz to zleep and captured me. She holdzzz me prizoner here to force my beezzz to work for her. They patrol the realm and alert her to any intruderzzz," Gwenyn told them sadly.

"How can we help you?" Octavia asked earnestly, looking at the tiny lock on the cage.

"Leave it to me!" squeaked Ferren. She leapt from Octavia's shoulder and onto the side of the cage; clutching at the bars, she peered into the lock. Rifling through her fur, she pulled out a tiny thorn that had got stuck there. She inserted the thorn into the lock and jiggled it around until with a click the cage door swung open.

"Thank you, Ferren of the quick handzzz!" Gwenyn flew from the cage, somersaulting in the air, finishing off with two laps of the room.

"Pleaze – I am in your debt, how can I repay you?" she asked the girls.

"Nesrin is holding our cousin here. We have to rescue her," Octavia told her. Gwenyn's antennae twitched angrily.

Lyffy croaked and headed into the room. "Whatever you do, do it quick; more guards are coming!"

Gwenyn stopped flying and, hovering in mid-air, began to buzz, louder and louder. Her song crescendoed as it was joined by a thousand more voices from outside the arched windows.

"Let them in," Gwenyn urged.

Octavia rushed to the latch and pushed the window open. She ducked as the cloud of bees entered the room and surrounded their queen in jubilation. Gwenyn buzzed out an order, and the swarm as one exited the room. Screams and shouts came from the hallway as the guards ran for their lives.

Eleven

Ad Astra

"THANK YOU, QUEEN GWENYN," Felicity said fervently; she grabbed her bow and arrow and headed for the door as well.

Octavia marvelled at her sister's new-found courage with pride. She quickly followed Felicity, along with Gwenyn and Lyffy.

"Which way shall we go?" she asked, checking the coast was still clear. She was relieved to see that the swarm of bees had created an impenetrable shield at either end of the corridor.

"I will lead you to the throne room; my beezzz will get the location of your couzin from Nezrin." Gwenyn led the way, her swarm parting like a curtain to let them through, their buzzing a soft, reassuring hum.

They climbed the black stone steps, embedded silver chips glistening in the light of the torches that lined the walls. A loud caw and a clap of thunder rolled across the ceiling above them, making them pause.

"That izzz juzt Taran, Nezrin'zzz raven; he izzz warning her."

They pressed on up the winding steps, finally bursting out into a magnificent hall, its roof open to the elements; a thousand stars glittered overhead, whilst the moon hung heavy in the sky.

Turning in a circle, Octavia took in the jet-black walls adorned with banners of black and silver. Two silver thrones sat on a raised platform, flanked with flaming torches burning purple.

The buzzing of the bees started getting louder as another crack rocked the room, throwing Octavia and Felicity to the floor. Pushing herself up onto her knees, Octavia saw a cloud floating down from the open roof. Nesrin stood upon it, her face livid; her staff was pointed directly at Gwenyn. Taran beadily eyed the queen bee from Nesrin's shoulder.

"How did you escape?!" Nesrin seethed with fury, indifferent to the angry mass of bees starting to surround her.

"That izzz no concern of yourzzz," Gwenyn said, flying up near Nesrin's face, and she buzzed out a command. Her bees swarmed Nesrin, who screamed shrilly; Taran flew up and out of the roofless hall, cawing loudly. A flash of light and a bang had Octavia and Felicity clutching each other. Smoke began to fill the room, and the bees started dropping one by one.

"Noooo!" Gwenyn shouted. She dove at Nesrin, who swatted her away with her staff. Gwenyn hit the wall heavily and slid down to lie crumpled on the floor, her tiny crown flying off and landing near Octavia. Ferren quickly scampered out of her pocket and grabbed the crown; unseen by Nesrin, she darted over to Gwenyn, who did not stir.

The cloud slowly descended. Nesrin stepped off and walked toward the girls, who stood up on trembling legs. She wagged her staff at them.

"Tut tut," she said. "Breaking into my castle, releasing my prisoners and attacking my guards – that is treason, my dears."

"You have our cousin. We want Beatrice back!" Octavia shouted, sounding braver than she felt. Standing her ground, she raised her chin in defiance.

"I have taken a liking to the girl; she will be the Princess of Castle Astra," Nesrin told them, circling them like a hungry shark, her teeth gleaming in the torchlight.

Out of the corner of her eye, Octavia could see Lyffy climbing up the pole that held one of the flaming torches. When he'd reached the top, he made a great leap and yelled, "Now!"

Felicity grabbed her bow and arrow and aimed it at Nesrin, who narrowed her eyes; the arrow shot from the bow and ricocheted off the staff just as Lyffy landed on the queen's head with a wet splat. She gave an outraged yell and put up both her hands, trying to claw off the toad. Her staff fell to the floor with a clatter. Octavia kicked it out of reach and went to help Lyffy, who was desperately trying to cling on.

Nesrin stumbled blindly into Octavia and fell to the floor with a thud; she tried to scream for her raven, but one of Lyffy's feet was in her mouth. She retched and spluttered furiously when she saw who her attacker was. "You!" she spat. "I thought I had dealt with you!"

Lyffy sneered, "I have been waiting for my chance."

Now that the smoke had cleared, the bees had started to awaken. They buzzed angrily as they saw a groggy Gwenyn being supported by Ferren on the floor. Gwenyn, her black eyes half open, buzzed out a faint command. The bees surrounded Nesrin and lifted her up as she screamed in protest. They started to carry her off when Gwenyn let out a startled buzz.

Octavia whipped around and was horrified to see Beatrice aiming Nesrin's fallen staff at Gwenyn and Ferren. She was dressed in a long black gown, shot through with silver thread. A circlet of stars sat atop her loose blonde hair.

"Bea!" Felicity shouted, as Octavia started forward toward her cousin. "What are you doing?"

"Stay back, or I will hurt them! My queen has been giving me lessons in staff magic," Beatrice said in a

monotone voice.

"She is starstruck – enchanted!" Lyffy croaked.

"You will release the queen, take your creatures, and leave," Beatrice told them, her eyes hazy.

"We are not leaving you here!" Octavia shouted desperately. "Please, Bea, come back with us, back to Martha. Don't you want to go home?" She took a tentative step toward Beatrice, who shuddered, her eyes flicking briefly to Octavia's.

"Go – please go! I do not want to hurt you." Beatrice's voice had taken on a strained tone, as if she was trying to fight an internal battle. Her hand trembled on the staff, but she didn't release her grip.

Felicity whispered to Octavia, "We can come back with help; we are out of our depth here."

Octavia shook her head violently. She couldn't leave Beatrice here – she wouldn't! She looked at Ferren, who twitched her whiskers helplessly.

A small lightning bolt landed at Octavia and Felicity's feet, where it sizzled on the black stone floor. Yelping in shock, Octavia jumped back. Devastated, she saw that Beatrice's eyes were once again blank.

"Go!" Beatrice shrieked, her tortured voice echoing around the room before it was sucked up and away into the starry sky.

In the ensuing silence, Lyffy waddled over to Ferren and helped support Gwenyn, who was slowly regaining her strength. She buzzed to her bees, who placed a heavily stung Nesrin onto the floor and came over to her side. On Gwenyn's request, they flew together, transforming into a platform.

"Ztep on; they will tranzport you back to Caztle Enfyzzz," Gwenyn told the girls weakly.

With one last beseeching look at Beatrice, Octavia bent to pick up Ferren and Gwenyn, whom she gently cradled in her arms. Felicity took Octavia's arm and helped her step onto the carpet of bees. Lyffy jumped onto Felicity's quiver and clung on with his webbed hands and feet.

A solitary tear tracked its way down Beatrice's face as she watched the bees rise. Nearby, Nesrin struggled to her feet and put out her hand for her staff.

"We will come back for you!" Octavia promised as they rose out of the castle and into the night sky, out of reach of Nesrin's magic. Nesrin's scream of fury followed them as they rose above the clouds.

They flew so high, Octavia thought they were travelling amongst the stars. In spite of the beauty around her, she watched Castle Astra disappear with a heavy heart. Felicity squeezed her hand as they sat on the cushion of bees, their furry bodies softly vibrating.

"You tried your bezt, but knowing when to retreat and regroup izzz nothing to be azhamed of," Gwenyn told them quietly.

"Thank you for helping us, Queen Gwenyn," Octavia said to the bee. "Your bees are very brave! Even knowing they would die, they still attacked and stung Nesrin."

"What do you mean?" Gwenyn replied, seeming confused.

"Bees die when they sting someone, don't they?"

Gwenyn gave a little chuckle. "You forget – you're in Fairy Land now. Thingzzz work a little differently here. It izzz all part of the magic. We are magical beingzzz, and something like uzing their ztingers will not kill *my* beezzz," she said proudly.

Octavia pondered this, before directing a question at Ferren. "If we shrink to fairy size when we come through the door, how are you animals all so small too? You are all mostly the size that you would be if I were to come across you in the woods at home."

"We are fairy creatures; our world is like a miniature version of yours, just with magic," Ferren explained simply, echoing what Evony had said earlier. "But the companion magic will allow me to grow to the size of a normal animal in your world. After all, what good would I be as a companion if you could barely see me, let alone hear me?"

Octavia nodded in understanding, eager to learn more about this magical realm.

Ferren continued, "But when fairies visit your world, they stay their tiny size in order to move undetected through your world to do their nightly work."

The group fell silent as Octavia let all the information sink in.

Lyffy stirred uncomfortably. "You can put me down outside the castle," he croaked gruffly.

"But I'm sure Queen Rhosyn will want to thank you for your help," Felicity told him, puzzled.

"The queen won't want to see me," he replied stubbornly, turning his back and watching the Middling Grounds far below.

Octavia shrugged her shoulders as she gazed at the stars overhead. A shooting star arced across the sky, and she wished with all her heart that they would be able to save Beatrice and return home as a family.

"I can't wait to see Mum; I hope she is all right," Felicity murmured after a while.

Octavia looked down to see that they were flying over Rhosyn's Woods. Castle Enfys was coming into view, shining like a beacon in the moonlight.

"Me too," she murmured back.

There was a warning shout from the castle as the guards reacted to the cloud of bees heading their way.

Octavia shouted out, "It is us – the Bloom girls!" She peered over the edge and saw Feargal on the platform. He recognised her immediately.

"Guards, stand down," he commanded.

The swarm gently lowered the girls onto the platform and hovered over Gwenyn, who buzzed out a command. The bees gave a buzz of assent and flew off.

"I have told them to find zome nectar and to rezt. I will call them back when I'm ztrong enough to go home,"

she explained to the girls.

"Please, will you take us to our mother?" Felicity asked Feargal, who was eyeing their dirty attire with a raised eyebrow.

"That was some entrance," he said sardonically, before bristling at them, paws on hips. "Do you know how worried everyone has been? The queen sent me on a rainbow to collect you from the marsh – you can imagine how I felt when you were nowhere to be found!"

Octavia and Felicity looked down at their feet in shame, and Octavia said quietly, "We're so sorry. We thought we would take a look at Castle Astra before waiting for the rainbow."

Feargal looked taken aback at this. "You went to Castle Astra! Come, I will take you to Queen Rhosyn; you can explain to her your serious lack of common sense." He started walking, then paused. "You can come too," he said, looking down his long snout at Lyffy, who was trying to slide out of view.

They followed Feargal to the throne room, passing the grand hall, where fairies and creatures dressed in dazzling gowns and tunics eyed them curiously from within, the celebrations for the Late Summer Ceremony still going strong.

Inside the throne room, Evony was anxiously pacing the floor but rushed to their side when they entered the room.

"Octavia! Felicity! Where have you been? Did you

complete the Quest – did you get the flower?" she asked breathlessly.

"We did. I sent it back using the box. Felicity was amazing! She defeated the wyvern," Octavia told her, but all she could feel was a sense of anti-climax and worry. They had come here to save one member of their family, but ended up risking three more.

"Well done, girls. Oh, and don't worry – Martha and Soren are fine. Hevva was able to heal them from the slumbershroom sleep. She got to them in time. Martha is sitting with your mother," Evony added.

Felicity sighed with relief, and Octavia felt hope blossom in her chest, but she couldn't embrace it yet. There was still so much at stake.

Queen Rhosyn had risen from her throne at their arrival and slowly walked toward them, a frown marring her beautiful face. Octavia gulped before addressing her.

"When we realised Castle Astra was so close, we – I mean I – decided we should investigate with the help of Lyffy the toad—"

She broke off as Queen Rhosyn turned her violet gaze to the toad, who was still trying his best to hide. Queen Rhosyn's eyes turned wide, and the colour drained from her cheeks.

"I cannot believe it! All this time wondering where you had gone. We will talk later," she told him softly as the toad shrank back.

Curious, Octavia glanced from one to the other before

continuing, "We got into the castle and rescued Queen Gwenyn here – she helped us get to the throne room. Nesrin came and we tried to get her to give Beatrice back to us, but she refused. Beatrice has been enchanted. She told us to go, and we managed to escape with the help of Gwenyn's bees."

"Entering Nesrin's castle was a foolish but brave move. Nevertheless, you should have waited for the rainbow." Octavia nodded in shame at this statement from the queen. "If your cousin is enchanted, you will need a strong magic to counteract it. Your mother losing hope has affected the flowers in fairy land, causing an imbalance; my magic is losing power as a result." Queen Rhosyn's voice was grave. "If the balance is not restored, Nesrin will be able to defeat me and take over, and that will lead to dark times for both fairy and human alike. Imagine – no more good dreams, no more visits from the tooth fairy; children all over your world will become fearful and disheartened."

"We have found the last flower. If we get the cure made and Mum sees Otto, she will start to believe again, won't she?" Octavia asked, hope colouring her tone.

"I have faith that it will work. I will send you back to the human world; you must bring the cure back using the Fairy Door and key. I will send Haf with you. She will help make the cure, and Ferren can go with you this once, but she must come back to Fairy Land until your Key Keeper Ceremony." Queen Rhosyn placed a comforting hand on Octavia's shoulder. "So young, but so brave," she murmured. "Our first step is to get your mother believing again so my power can be restored; then we can save your cousin."

"May I see Mum before I go back?"

Queen Rhosyn looked at her compassionately. "Of course," she said, and spoke to Evony. "Would you please take them to their mother, then bring Octavia to the portal chamber? But first – Briar, please refresh the Bloom daughters' attire."

Briar rushed forward from her place at the foot of the throne. She looked askance at the girls' messy appearance and quickly used her wand to change their clothes and clean their hair.

Nodding gratefully at Briar and leaving Gwenyn and Lyffy with the queen, Felicity and Octavia followed Evony from the room. She took them up the winding stairs past the room where Otto still slept. Octavia glanced at it, feeling a sudden burst of happiness that soon her brother would be able to come home, but the feeling faded as rapidly as it had come when she thought of Beatrice. Ferren peeped out of her pocket and regarded her with sad eyes, as if sensing her swirling emotions.

Evony was opening the door to the room above Otto's, so Octavia hastened to catch up.

Mum lay asleep upon a curtained bed, her pale face a sharp contrast to her bright hair. Martha sat on a chair underneath the window; she leapt up when she saw her

cousins.

"Beatrice?" she asked hopefully.

Octavia shook her head sadly. "We tried to save her. We even risked entering Nesrin's castle to do so, but she has been enchanted. If we get Mum believing again, Queen Rhosyn will be able to help us."

Martha's shoulders slumped, but she met Octavia's eyes and said, "I'm sorry for what I said in the Marsh – you are not to blame for this. I didn't have to come through the door. I was just so scared seeing Beatrice get taken." She held out her arms. Octavia ran gratefully into them and squeezed Martha back tightly.

"If we all work together, we will get Bea back," Octavia told her eldest cousin determinedly. Martha released her and nodded.

Felicity had gone to stand next to their mother; she gently clasped her hand. "Mum, can you hear me?" she asked softly.

Pan fluttered anxiously overhead. He chirped a quick hello to the girls before staring back down at Mum, whose eyes flickered open. She stared, unseeing, at the canopy above before turning her head. Seeing Felicity and Octavia, she gave a watery smile.

"My girls," she whispered huskily.

Octavia clasped her other hand. "We got it, Mum; we got the Arianthe flower! I sent it through to Grandmother," she told her, trying to inject enthusiasm into her voice.

Colour slowly bloomed in Mum's cheeks. "You did?

Oh, my clever girls." Taking a deep breath, she struggled to sit up.

Hevva started forward from the corner of the room. "You are still weak, Key Keeper. Silly humans, messing with fairy magic," she muttered brusquely, adjusting the pillow behind Mum's shoulders.

Mum looked at the old fairy wryly. "I know, but I couldn't sit back and leave all of my children and my nieces in danger," she responded guiltily. Looking around the room, she smiled at Martha. "Where is Beatrice?"

Martha opened her mouth to speak, but Evony cut across her with an almost imperceptible shake of her head. "She will be along soon," she told her.

"Mum, I have to go back to Castle Bloom and get the cure. When we wake Otto, that will help you heal too," Octavia said, glossing over the details. Kissing her gently on the cheek, she murmured, "I'll be back soon."

Mum frowned, but nodded. "Your father, aunt and uncle should be at Castle Bloom – they were on their way there when I got the crazy idea to try and come here using the dust. Pan did try to talk me out of it, but I wouldn't listen. I couldn't face your father and tell him we might have lost all of our children." She looked down. "This shouldn't have had to fall on you, but you have proven yourself many times, and I am proud of you – of all of you," she sniffed.

Octavia met Felicity's eyes. "Look after her. I will be back with the cure," she said in a determined voice.

She walked past Martha and gently patted her arm. Martha gave a wobbly smile in return. Without a backward glance, Octavia followed Evony from the room.

Twelve

Many Hands Make Light Work

EAVILY GUARDED, the Portal Chamber sat deep
in the castle dungeons. Evony guided Octavia
through the low doorway, where Queen Rhosyn
and Haf were waiting. Ordinarily Octavia would have been
bursting with questions about how the portal worked, but
she was so eager to get back home and make the cure that
she barely took in the marble room, which was empty
except for a crystal archway in the centre.

The queen nodded at Octavia and touched her staff
to the rainbow-coloured gem at the base of the arch. The
gem glowed and flickered for a moment before it winked
out. Queen Rhosyn inspected her staff with a worried
look and tried again. This time the gem stayed aglow, and
beams of coloured light shot out to connect with matching

stones all around the arch; the space between rippled with a fluid rainbow sheen.

Ferren squeaked and buried herself deep in Octavia's pocket, which Octavia patted reassuringly. Haf stepped up to stand next to Octavia.

"Bring back the cure. Our world depends upon it," Queen Rhosyn said as Octavia and Haf stepped through the archway together.

The queen's words ringing in her head, Octavia fell dizzily. Something fluttered past her face and she reached out to grab it, but it was just out of reach.

With a thud, she landed heavily on dusty floorboards. A startled cry had her whirling to the window. Moonlight shone through it, illuminating a silhouette curled up on the window seat.

"Octavia!" Grandmother cried, rushing to help her granddaughter to her feet.

"Grandmother! Did you get the flower?" Octavia demanded breathlessly. The 'something' was still fluttering around her face, and she tried to swat it away when an indignant voice stopped her.

"Key Keeper, it is me!"

Octavia looked to see Haf fluttering beside her, now the size of a hummingbird.

"Oh, Haf, I am so sorry," she exclaimed, before turning back to her grandmother, whose eyes had widened with shock at the sight of the little fairy.

She answered Octavia's question readily. "Yes – it

appeared outside the door a few hours ago. I gave it to your Great-Aunt Clara, who took it to your father – who is here, by the way, along with your aunt and uncle – I waited and waited, hoping you were all not far behind it. I have been so worried!" She ended on an accusatory note, frowning.

Octavia gave a great sigh of relief. "I am sorry to have caused you worry, Grandmother, but we had to help save Otto. Does Dad have all of the other flowers? We need the cure now!" she said, brushing off her leggings, which were a tangible reminder of Fairy Land.

"Yes, but what about the others?" Grandmother asked frantically, trying to keep up with Octavia as she headed out of the attic.

"Where is Dad? I'll fill you all in together," she said, rushing along, Haf fluttering anxiously behind her.

Grandmother followed Octavia, shouting at her retreating back. "They are in the hot-house."

Octavia burst into the hot-house at the back of the castle. Her father, his black hair standing up in tufts, looked up in shock.

"Octavia!" he shouted, rushing over to grab her in a great bear hug. Taking a moment to breathe in his familiar, comforting, earthy scent, she closed her eyes and sagged against him.

He gently released her. "Where is your mother?" he asked, looking behind her for the others.

"She's fine, or she will be when we get the cure back

to Otto – she was hurt using the dust and has lost hope which has had a dangerous effect on Fairy Land. If we don't get her believing again, and soon, Nesrin will take over," Octavia explained, the words tumbling out in a breathless rush.

Dad nodded grimly. "I should've been here; your mother shouldn't have had to deal with this alone." He clutched the edge of the work bench.

"You were getting the other flower; it was important you did so – now we have all we need," Octavia reassured him.

A bark and running feet sounded down the corridor.

"We were in the kitchen!" Aunt Anastasia said breathlessly as she skidded into the hot-house; grasping the door frame, she looked around for her daughters. Her husband ploughed into the back of her, he too frantically searching the room. Bronwen pranced in behind them and headed straight for Octavia.

Octavia's stomach plummeted into her feet, her hands becoming clammy at the thought of the news she still had to impart. Needing a minute to compose herself, she buried her face in Bronwen's fur and took a few deep breaths.

Straightening, she looked into her aunt's eyes, and took another deep breath. "Aunt Ana, Uncle Piers... Felicity, Martha and Beatrice are still in Fairy Land. Martha and Felicity are looking after Mum...." She trailed off.

"And Beatrice?" Uncle Piers asked, raking a trembling hand through his chestnut hair.

"Nesrin took her. She has bewitched her—"

Octavia broke off as Aunt Anastasia gave a strangled cry and sank to her knees. Uncle Piers put a hand to his mouth in horror and bent to clutch his wife, who was weeping, great racking sobs shaking her slim frame.

"We have to restore Queen Rhosyn's power by making the cure; that's the only way we can make Mum believe again," Octavia said earnestly. "If the Key Keeper believes, Fairy Land will become strong and healthy and Queen Rhosyn will become powerful again. She will not be able to beat Nesrin until she is at full power." She knelt next to her aunt, whose sorrow pulsed off her in waves.

Great-Aunt Clara, who had entered the room silently, bustled over. "Come on, Ana." She helped her niece to her feet and led her over to a battered sofa in the corner. Settling her, she announced, "We need tea!"

Grandmother, who had been standing by the door, left to find Mrs Fawcett. Octavia took a deep breath and prepared herself for a long night.

She introduced Haf and Ferren to her family. Haf went to help Dad and Uncle Piers work on the cure, poring over the parchment and reading the instructions in her tinkling little voice. Octavia, feeling helpless, sat next to her aunt, who clutched a full cup of tea for warmth and comfort. Bronwen padded over and laid her head in Aunt Anastasia's lap, her big, sorrowful eyes gazing up at her.

Grandmother looked worriedly at her daughter. "Ana, the quicker we create the cure, the quicker we can get Otto and Beatrice back," she told her gently.

"Bea," moaned Aunt Anastasia. She looked at Octavia. "Is that true? Can we get her back?"

"Yes, absolutely – we will not stop until the Bloom family is back together again!" Octavia told her confidently.

Aunt Anastasia took a deep breath before taking a sip of her tea. Firmly, she placed the cup onto the side table and, giving Bronwen a pat, stood with a little wobble and walked over to join her husband.

Great-Aunt Clara nodded proudly. "We Bloom girls are a strong bunch – Beatrice will be fine," she said, handing Rowan a biscuit. He split it in half and offered it to Ferren. Ferren nibbled gratefully and stared around the glass-panelled room, taking in her first sights of the human world.

"A mouse – I should've guessed that would be your companion. Creeping around at night and getting up to all sorts of mischief. Suits you perfectly." Grandmother sniffed, though a slight smile was playing around her lips.

Octavia exchanged a smile with Ferren. Yes, she was indeed perfect. She stroked the tiny mouse with affection. An overwhelming tiredness came over her; she looked at the full moon, which had dropped low in the sky, the first vestiges of dawn starting to colour the sky. Cushioning her head on her arm, she watched as Haf, her father, aunt and uncle stewed the petals of the seven flowers in different vats, mesmerised by the billowing, coloured smoke and sated by the intoxicating aromas they gave off.

"You won't win, you know," said Nesrin idly.

She sat on her silver throne, Beatrice at her side. Octavia was trapped in a bubble which hovered in Nesrin's roofless hall. Nesrin used her staff to gently bounce the bubble up and down, causing Octavia to lose her balance. Falling to her knees, she clawed at the bubble until it popped; heavily, she fell the few feet to the floor and Nesrin cackled mercilessly.

"You're wrong!" Furious, Octavia staggered to her feet, pushing her copper braids out of her face and glaring at Nesrin, who flicked her staff at her, an amused smile on her haughty face. Octavia was forced to dance out of the way of mini lightning bolts as they seared her leather shoes.

Out of breath, she darted behind a black onyx pillar.

"We're coming for you, Bea, but you have to fight her!" she called. "Fight! Figh...! Fi...!"

"It's done!"

Dad's jubilant voice awoke Octavia. The sun had come up and its watery light was starting to fill the room. Octavia, her heart in her mouth, was disorientated. She stared around the room and met Haf's worried gaze.

"The Arianthe flower's fumes can cause vivid dreams. Are you all right?" the fairy asked her.

Octavia nodded slowly. *Just a dream – or was it?* Shaking her head to clear the last of the worrying visions, she got to her feet and stretched, walking over to Dad. Great-Aunt Clara snored noisily in a patched-up armchair in the corner. Rowan rolled his squirrel eyes and went back to licking his tail.

Grandmother put out her arm and gave Octavia a brief hug as she passed by; surprised, Octavia met her eyes. Seeing pride and admiration in their aged gaze, she smiled, feeling close to her grandmother for the first time.

Seven vials stood on the work bench, each a differing colour of the rainbow. Her father stood next to them, beaming, sweat glistening on his brow.

"Well done," tinkled Haf. "Now comes the tricky part: all seven must be poured at the same time. It must be done correctly, or it will not work at all," she added warningly.

Octavia looked around and counted. "Seven vials, seven people," she mused. "Well, one fairy," she corrected herself, with a smile at Haf.

Dad looked at Grandmother. "You'd better wake Clara; we need all hands on deck for this," he said, rolling

up his sleeves.

Grandmother bustled over to Great-Aunt Clara, whilst Dad decided who would have which flower vial.

"Red Fire Lily for you, Ana; Orange Fire Poppy for you, Piers; Evelyn, you can take the Yellow Rothchild's Slipper Orchid; Clara" – who sleepily rubbed her eyes and yawned – "you can take the Green Jade Vine; Haf, can you manage the Blue Kadupul Flower? And I'll take the Indigo Corpse Flower." He looked at Octavia seriously. "Which leaves you with the Violet Arianthe Flower – which is only fitting, I think."

Octavia looked at the violet liquid swirling in the glass vial, her fingers tingling again.

"Right. Lift your vials, and on the count of three, pour it into the bowl," Dad instructed, looking around to make sure everyone agreed. Seeing the nods, he picked up his vial and watched whilst everyone followed suit. Haf struggled with hers; her wings fluttering furiously, she only just managed to pick up the vial in her arms.

"One, two, three," Dad counted, and in unison everyone poured their liquid into the crystal bowl.

The colours swirled together, forming a rainbow. Following the instructions, Dad stirred it seven times clockwise and seven times anticlockwise. As the last drop dripped off the ladle and back into the bowl, the mixture had turned golden. The heady aroma of a meadow filled the hot-house and mingled with the scents already coming from the flowers and plants in the room.

Everyone stared into the bowl, and an overwhelming sense of relief came over Octavia. Dad hastened to ladle the mixture into glass bottles; handing one to Octavia, he gave her a swift hug.

"Take this to your mother and cure Otto," he told her. "We'll keep the rest of the cure safe for any future boy babies. Evelyn?" He gave the other bottles to Grandmother, who took them over to a locked glass cabinet.

Octavia placed her bottle into her tunic pocket along with Ferren. "Great-Aunt Clara, will you help me reveal the door?" she asked. "I only managed to do it last time with Felicity's help."

Great-Aunt Clara nodded. "Of course – you are not yet ten. Felicity being a future Guardian must have boosted your Key Keeper power. When you reach ten, all you will need to do is swipe your hand across the skirting board and it will be revealed," she explained, "but I'll do it this time." She led the way to the attic, Rowan sitting on her shoulder like a pirate's parrot. The others followed behind. The sun was fully up now and blazed through the arched stone windows, warming the usually cold passageways.

Uncle Piers and Aunt Anastasia were arguing quietly at the back.

"I want to go through with Octavia and help rescue Beatrice," Aunt Anastasia was whispering vehemently.

"I can't lose you too, Ana!" Uncle Piers was adamant.

Haf piped up squeakily, "I am sorry, but Queen

Rhosyn has asked me to convey that Octavia alone should come back through; Nesrin will be monitoring the toadstool ring, on the lookout for any Fairy Door activity, and the fewer humans that come through, the less she will hopefully notice." She looked apologetically at Aunt Anastasia, who stopped walking and began sobbing quietly. Uncle Piers wrapped his arms around her.

"I have faith in Octavia," Grandmother said quietly as they grouped in the centre of the attic. Standing in the warm pool of sunlight, she looked deep into her granddaughter's surprised eyes. "Get the cure to your mother; make her believe again."

Octavia gave a determined nod and looked at Great-Aunt Clara, who walked over to the skirting board. She bent stiffly and ran her hand over the old wood. Everyone watched as the Fairy Door slowly solidified once again – gleaming golden still, but the flowers around it now wilted and brown. Great-Aunt Clara exchanged a worried look with Grandmother, who placed a comforting hand on Aunt Anastasia's back.

"Be safe, my daughter," Dad whispered.

"I will. I'll bring them all back – I promise." Octavia looked into her aunt's sad eyes as she said the last part. Aunt Anastasia gave a thin smile and clutched Uncle Piers.

Octavia looked at her family in turn, committing their faces to memory. From underneath her tunic, she pulled out the vine necklace and retrieved the tiny key. On a deep breath, she inserted it into the lock, and with an almost imperceptible click the miniature door swung open. She held out her hand, and Haf stepped onto it.

Prepared this time, Octavia welcomed the bubble-like sensation, willing herself into Fairy Land.

Thirteen

Best-Laid Plans

OISED FOR ATTACK, Octavia scanned the meadow. She stepped out from the Fairy Ring and looked at Haf, who pointed at the entrance to Rhosyn's Woods. Aurus waited there, his golden coat gleaming in the dappled sunlight.

"Watch out!" he shouted as a dark shape swooped from the sky. Octavia put her hands up and ducked. Taran cawed in frustration and wheeled around to dive again, thunder rolling despite the cloudless sky.

Aurus came bounding out of the wood. "Get on!" he shouted, and Octavia grabbed his thick fur, swinging herself onto his back. She clasped Haf's hand, and the fairy slid gratefully behind her onto Aurus' broad back. He took off, racing into Rhosyn's Woods.

Taran beat his wings in the air, thunder booming with every flap as he was repelled by Queen Rhosyn's magic boundary.

"I am not sure how long the defences will last; we need to keep going!" Aurus shouted as he thundered through the mossy tracks, throwing up pieces of dirt in his wake, and over the bridge; bubbles popped around them as the Stream of Dreams passed underneath.

They exited the wood at a run and nearly knocked over Feargal, who was waiting with a transportation bubble. Octavia slid from Aurus' back on shaky legs and patted his pelt in thanks.

Breathing heavily, Aurus said, "You will be safe now." He bowed his majestic head and trotted off down the hill toward the castle to the guard's entrance.

"Your carriage, milady," Feargal said sarcastically with a quirky little bow. His eyes twinkled mischievously as Octavia let out a shout of laughter, still buoyed up on adrenaline.

"Oh, it's good to be back," she told him as she entered the bubble and sat, Haf following with a censorious look at Feargal.

Checking that Ferren and the cure were still safe, Octavia watched as the bubble approached the castle. This was it. What she had set out to do was finally in her grasp; it all rested on the tiny crystal bottle in her pocket.

The bubble landed on the platform with a couple of gentle bounces. Evony was once again waiting to greet

Octavia, this time with Felicity anxiously standing beside her. As soon as Octavia disembarked, Felicity ran over.

"Tavi, you made it back! Do you have the cure?" she asked in a rush, hugging her so tightly that Ferren squeaked indignantly.

"Careful!" Octavia said with a laugh. She put her hand in her pocket and retrieved the bottle, while Ferren ran up her arm to sit on her shoulder. "We only narrowly made it back – Taran was waiting for us!"

Evony stepped forward. "Nesrin will indeed do all she can to stop you, but well done, Key Keeper; you have passed your quest." She bowed low with respect. "Now, let's go to your mother."

Mum was propped up in bed, gently having her hair brushed by Martha. She had more colour in her cheeks, and her eyes lit up when Octavia rushed in.

"Mum, I have it – I have the cure!" She thrust the bottle into her mother's hand. Mum gazed at the golden liquid and one tear rolled slowly down her cheek. She clutched at Octavia's hand.

"Oh, my precious, clever girl."

"I couldn't have done it without the others. We are a great team, we Bloom girls!" Octavia smiled at Felicity and Martha proudly. Felicity smiled back, but Martha,

her features pale, only nodded sadly.

"Here, take it to Hevva – she will administer it to Otto." Mum handed the bottle back to Octavia and squeezed her hand.

Octavia linked her arm with Felicity's, and together they walked back down the stairs to Otto's room. Aloysius was, surprisingly, alert and standing to attention; he eyed them beadily as they made to walk past him.

"None may pass without the queen's consent," he growled, placing his spear in front of the door.

Hevva opened the door and glared at the badger. "What's all this nonsense? I told you to let the Key Keeper in when she returns," she admonished.

"Just doing my duty," he huffed, lowering the spear and letting the girls pass by.

Octavia stared at Otto, who still lay peacefully on the bed. Wordlessly, she handed the bottle to Hevva, who inspected it closely. The gold liquid swirled, gleaming in the torchlight. Satisfied, Hevva walked over to the bedside and removed two crystals. Immediately, the sleep mist cleared.

Octavia watched in wonder as her brother slowly opened his violet-blue eyes and looked around the room. His eyes locked with hers and he grinned.

"Tavi, you came!" he said, his voice husky.

"Of course! You're our brother – we couldn't leave you here!" Octavia told him, grinning back.

Felicity stepped to Octavia's side. "I'm Felicity," she

told Otto with a shy smile.

"Hi, Fliss," he replied happily, already using her nickname.

"Here, young man: take your medicine." Hevva sat him up and held the vial to his lips.

Otto sniffed it apprehensively, but gamely took a huge gulp. He immediately began to glow; rainbow colours arced from his skin, lighting him from within. He shuddered once, twice, then lay still. The glow receded until he was back to his normal self, copper curls falling haphazardly across his brow and mischievous eyes twinkling.

"Can I go home now?" he asked simply. Octavia and Felicity rushed across the room to jump on the bed. They crushed him in an exuberant hug.

"Gently, girls!" Hevva tutted, but Otto was laughing uproariously and hugging them back with glee.

"What's all this noise?" a breathless voice asked from the doorway. All three turned to see their mother clutching at the doorway for support, tears of happiness running down her face. Pan swooped through the doorway and whooped happily as he saw the three children.

"What are you doing out of bed? You do not have your full strength back yet!" Hevva rushed over to support Mum to the rocking chair.

"I feel wonderful." Mum sniffled, gazing at Otto, her eyes drinking in the sight of him.

"Hmm... you do look better," Hevva conceded,

passing her a cup. "Drink this. It will finish your healing process."

Mum sipped the drink, and took several moments to gaze at the three children together and safe. Her eyes were sparkling again and her cheeks had a healthy glow.

Evony came fluttering through the door. "There you are, Genevieve! I knew you must be feeling better – the unicorns are in full bloom. My mother has regained her powers; we advance to Castle Astra tonight!"

And with those words, the peaceful moment passed.

Mum, Octavia, Otto, Felicity and Martha retired to the Amethyst room for a light lunch and a rest before they had an audience with the queen.

"So, you never knew about me? At all?" Otto asked Octavia as they sat on the window seat together.

"No – I had no idea until I dreamt about you. Did you dream about me too?" Octavia asked. Ferren listened avidly, accepting berries from Otto.

"Only that once. I knew about you, of course – Hevva woke me from time to time to give me various potions and she would tell me stories. The queen wanted me to be prepared for when I came home. I always had faith I *would* come home; I knew I had to meet you!" Otto mirrored Octavia's own giant smile.

"Come and have more honey cakes, you two. We will need our strength for later," Mum called over. Although she smiled, too, it didn't reach her eyes.

Otto jumped off the seat and ran over to her. Stopping for a brief hug, he snatched a few cakes and tossed one to Octavia, who caught it with a laugh. She broke off a piece and held it out to Pan, who was eyeing it hopefully.

"Don't give Pan any more. I think he has had quite enough," Mum said, and looked pointedly at the bird's rounded stomach. Octavia giggled and finished off the rest of the cake herself.

Martha watched the exchange quietly; she was toying with the compass under her tunic. Mum looked over at her.

"We will get her back, Matty, I promise. Now you need to eat," she coaxed gently.

Martha managed a few nibbles before pushing her plate away. Mum eyed her sadly for a moment before speaking to Octavia.

"Whilst I remember, I will look after the key for now. Don't look so sad – it will be returned to you on your tenth birthday," she added with a laugh as Octavia reluctantly pulled the vine necklace over her head and handed it to her mother.

A knock at the door made them jump. Mum went over to answer it.

"The queen will see you now," Briar told them.

A surprise awaited them in the throne room: a tall, handsome male fairy sat in the throne next to the queen; his moss-green and gold eyes twinkled sardonically at the girls. Octavia started; those eyes looked oddly familiar.

Queen Rhosyn noticed Octavia staring, whilst Evony looked amused.

"Please may I introduce my husband, King Llyffant."

The king inclined his head. His long, green hair was swept back off his face and tied with a vine. He had magnificent green-and-gold-speckled wings.

"Lyffy?" squeaked Ferren from Octavia's shoulder in surprise. Octavia looked again into those green-gold eyes and smiled. *Of course! Lyffy.*

"Welcome, Otto, you who know only too well the devastation one of Nesrin's curses can wreak. Well, we too have been afflicted – Nesrin was in love with King Llyffant, but he was betrothed to me." Queen Rhosyn bestowed a loving smile on her husband. "When Evony was younger, the king took her into the meadow to practise archery. Nesrin came upon them and turned the king into a toad in her jealousy and anger. In his shame, he left to live in my woods, though we looked for him and never gave up hope. I have to thank you Bloom girls for reuniting us."

"But how did you cure him?" Octavia blurted, and then flushed at her outburst.

"The purest medicine in the world – love," Queen Rhosyn said simply. King Llyffant raised her hand to his lips and kissed it respectfully. He looked at Octavia.

"You have my sincerest gratitude, Octavia Bloom; my pride always did get the best of me. I needed to have faith that true love always wins." He winked a slow, amphibian-like wink.

Octavia smiled back delightedly, and exchanged a knowing look with her mother.

"Now, to business!" Queen Rhosyn announced, waving her staff. A large, circular crystal table appeared, surrounded by golden chairs. "Please be seated," she told the assembled crowd.

An assortment of strong-looking fairies and creatures took their seats. Aurus nodded to Octavia from across the table where he stood, and Queen Gwenyn buzzed a hello from a tiny throne on the table.

"Thanks to our human friends here, our flowers are blooming once more," the queen began. "Our spies have tracked the fire imps to the Middling Grounds, where they await Nesrin's orders. Martha will lead the guard with Aurus, using her compass." Martha jumped in her seat at her name; she dazedly looked around the group of warriors and trackers, and gulped nervously. "Evony, Felicity and the archers will space themselves throughout the group. Queen Gwenyn's bees will scout from the skies, whilst the king, myself and the remaining Blooms will bring up the rear. Feargal, you will remain here with a small guard to protect Castle Enfys and the remaining fairy court," Queen Rhosyn instructed.

Shouts, neighs, grunts, buzzes and bellows of assent echoed around the table, to which the queen nodded imperiously. "Go and collect your weapons and supplies; we ride within the hour," she told them.

Chairs were scraped back, and hooves and claws clattered on the stone floor as the room was vacated. Octavia gazed pensively around at Otto, her mother, Martha, Felicity and Evony in the ensuing silence.

Otto was bouncing in his seat, ready for action. The queen smiled at him affectionately and said, "I have a gift for you, Bloom son. This shield may look small, but its reach is mighty. Hold it above you, and it will shield not only you but those around you," she told him.

Awestruck, he received the gift and said, "Thank you, Your Majesty."

"It has been a pleasure having you here, but I am pleased you will be going home." She turned to look solemnly at Martha. "I pledge to you, Bloom daughter, that you will *all* be going home safely." She held out her hand. Martha took it tentatively and watched as a rainbow bloomed from their entwined hands. Martha's eyes widened and a happy smile grew across her face; she met the queen's eyes and, after a searching moment, nodded.

"And finally, Key Keeper," Queen Rhosyn addressed Mum, "your biggest gift, and weapon, is to believe and have hope. Our land has been reliant on the faith and

belief of humans for millennia; over time that belief has diminished as humans forgot about magic. But you, our last true believers, with the traces of fairy magic in your veins, make us stronger."

Mum looked around at her children and niece and smiled. "I believe in them and in the magic of this land, and I have hope that you will get Beatrice back," she said as Pan nodded his head in agreement from his perch on her shoulder. She stood and curtseyed to the queen and king in turn. *Not a wobble in sight,* Octavia thought proudly.

"Sorrel will take you to the kitchen to gather supplies." The queen dismissed them with a smile.

The kitchen was a whirl of activity as garden fairies and food fairies hurried to put together enough supplies to feed the army. The girls and Otto watched as pots and pans floated through the air and packages of food wrapped themselves all under the orchestration of a plump, matronly, extremely old fairy with faded red hair.

Sorrel took them over to her. "Cegin, this is the Bloom family from the human world. Please supply them with necessary sustenance for the journey ahead," she said.

Cegin eyed them over the top of her waving hands, her wand a blur. Without missing a beat, several packages

sailed over to land in a neat pile in Mum's arms. With a surprised laugh, Mum handed out the packages to the children, who placed them in their bags. Bottles of elderflower water flowed in an arc, narrowly missing Pan, who was fluttering above Mum's head, over to the group, who plucked them one by one out of the air. Pan gave an indignant chirp and settled on the safety of Mum's shoulder, where she stroked him placatingly.

"Thank you!" the children chorused and were given a terse nod from the fairy, who went back to her ministrations.

They left the hustle and bustle of the kitchen and followed Sorrel up and out into the courtyard. They blinked in the bright sunlight; the sun was high in the sky and warmed their faces as they walked over to the assembled group.

King Llyffant nodded to Octavia as she took her position at the rear with Otto and her mother. They stood next to the queen's hare, Eira, who twitched her whiskers at them in greeting. Octavia stared at the regal-looking hare in admiration.

Evony, who was passing by, noticed Octavia staring. "Eira is beautiful, isn't she? She can create snow!" she told her. Octavia's eyes widened, and Evony smiled.

"Wow," Octavia breathed. "I did wonder if she had any magical gifts, because Nesrin's raven Taran can create thunder," she added thoughtfully.

"You're very perceptive." Evony nodded. "Technically,

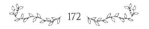

Nesrin should not have a magical companion – they are only for the true queen or king of Fairy Land – but my mother struck a bargain with Nesrin to try to quell her thirst for power. Sadly, it did not work."

Octavia nodded eagerly. "I would love to hear more about that," she said, hoping for another fairy story.

Mum laughed before Evony could reply. "You and your fairy tales! I don't think this is a good time," she reminded her daughter, as Queen Rhosyn stopped talking with one of her advisors and shot a rainbow from her staff to garner attention.

Felicity gave brief hugs to her family and, hoisting her quiver of arrows, followed Evony to the centre of the troupe. Martha gave a small wave and headed to the front, where she was welcomed by Aurus.

Queen Rhosyn nodded in satisfaction as all eyes turned upon her. She looked down from her seat upon the largest unicorn Octavia had ever seen. It bloomed with golden flowers, which sparkled like liquid gold in the sun's bright rays.

"We will head into Bloomsville Village, where those of you without hoof will collect their unicorns." To a rousing cheer, the golden gates were thrown open and a crystal bridge was revealed, from which a winding path snaked into the village.

The rest of the Fairy Court waved flags and blew tinkling trumpets as the party exited Castle Enfys and headed toward battle.

Fourteen

Flight of the Bumble Bea

SOREN AND FINNIAN WERE WAITING in the town square with a herd of vibrantly blooming unicorns. Soren's eyes rounded when he saw the king; a collective gasp swept through the villagers, followed by a ripple effect as fairies bent in a fluid bow at his passing. King Llyffant smiled and nodded as he rode along on his own bronze-flowered unicorn.

Finnian hurried over and breathlessly assigned unicorns to those who needed them. Otto was given Oren, a lively unicorn blooming with bright orange flowers, while Mum paired with Fides, a beautiful mare with brown blooms. Octavia was overjoyed to be reunited with Xanthe, who was glowing with renewed colour.

Martha seemed lost for words as Aurus approached

her, leading Linnea and Caeruleus.

"For Beatrice," he said gruffly, nodding at the blue unicorn, who turned sombre eyes on her. Octavia rubbed her cousin's arm in support as she watched the exchange.

"Thank you, Aurus," Martha said when she found her voice. Octavia could see the hope shining in her cousin's eyes, and wished fervently that they would indeed be returning with Beatrice alongside them, riding the large stallion.

Soren approached the king and queen, whilst his father looked on nervously. "May I offer my services again? I would be honoured to accompany you and assist with the unicorns," he said. Bowing low, he gave a quick sideways glance at Evony, which was not missed by the king.

King Llyffant pursed his lips and regarded the fairy for a moment, then looked at the queen with a raised eyebrow. After a silent interchange, the king nodded.

"Very well, young Soren; you may come."

"Thank you, Your Majesty." Soren backed away and swung onto Ember, who reared in anticipation.

"Show-off," Evony muttered, but her tone didn't quite match the look on her face. She caught Octavia's grinning face and, flushing, looked away.

Everyone once again took up their positions within the troupe and waited expectantly.

"Martha, Aurus, please lead on!" the queen commanded. The group left the village and headed into

the dappled coolness of Rhosyn's Woods.

"So, do I get a companion too?" Otto asked, looking at Ferren and Pan as they sat on Octavia's and Mum's shoulders. All three rode side-by-side along the wide track. Octavia looked questioningly at their mum, who looked puzzled.

"I really don't know," she said. "Two children born in the same generation with copper curls and violet-blue eyes has never occurred before." The track narrowed, and she was forced to steer Fides ahead of the twins.

"Maybe I should ask the queen." Otto craned his neck to look behind him at Queen Rhosyn, who was deep in conversation with the king and a large eagle.

"Probably not the best time," Octavia told him, manoeuvring Xanthe around a fallen log.

They watered their unicorns and filled water bottles in the same glistening stream at the edge of the woods before forging on past the Flower Fields, where garden fairies and forest fairies were working together to nurture the newly growing seedlings. They stopped briefly to shout well-wishes and wave their aprons like flags as the troupe passed.

As the company approached the Middling Grounds, the archers nocked their arrows and Queen Gwenyn ordered her bees upward to look for signs of ambush, but all was still. They passed through the area uneventfully; nothing stirred, yet the air was heavy and cloying. They forged on – making good time, as the healthy, blooming

unicorns pranced on swiftly – and decided to make camp and discuss their plan of attack at the edge of Misty Marsh. In the distance, Castle Astra could be glimpsed shining brightly on its cliff.

They made camp in a raised clearing above the swamp, where jagged stone steps led from the swamp and continued up a huge wall of stone behind in jutted ledges. A dark waterfall fell into a pool at the bottom. A wise-looking fairy tested the water and deemed it safe to drink from.

Black clouds started to roll in, and thunder boomed ominously in the distance. Evony scanned the skies and seemed satisfied before directing Soren to take the unicorns to the pool to drink. Gwenyn's bees surrounded the camp, a buzzing net of protection.

Martha and Felicity came to sit with Octavia and Otto. Felicity showed the others her arrows. "Evony just gave these to me – they've been dipped in sleep dust to knock out our enemies. Then we can capture them easily!" she said.

Octavia looked with interest at the arrows, but stopped when Mum narrowed her eyes. "Please be careful with those! We don't need any more of us succumbing to enchanted sleeps."

Nodding sheepishly, Octavia helped Mum split a large loaf of bread five ways, which she handed out with cups full of fat, juicy blackberries. Pan flitted around Mum's head until she held up a chunk of bread; he swooped low and nipped it from her fingers.

"Thanks," he mumbled through his full beak, settling next to Ferren, who was nibbling a berry delicately.

"Cheeky bird," Mum chuckled.

The king and queen retired to their tent with their warrior chiefs. For a few peaceful moments Octavia watched tendrils of mist snake along the ground whilst sipping her peppermint tea.

Out of nowhere, tension surrounded the camp. The hairs rose on the back of Octavia's arms; she gathered Ferren close and noted Mum doing the same with Pan, tucking him into her pocket. Octavia looked around at her family as the light-hearted conversation stopped and everyone looked up, sensing there was something wrong.

There was a moment of eerie silence, then a sudden shockwave ripped through the camp. Creatures and fairies alike were tossed into the sky like broken toys, and stunned bees rained from the sky, hitting the ground heavily. Mum gave a yell and pulled Octavia and Otto down, while Martha and Felicity ducked.

Queen Rhosyn fought her way out of her tent as it exploded around her, her fury visible as she propelled herself forward on her large wings. She hoisted her staff and pointed it into the falling throng, stopping their descent. Unconscious fairies and animals hung like puppets on invisible wires.

"I can't hold them much longer," she shouted through gritted teeth. Her hand shook on the staff, her knuckles

white with the effort.

King Llyffant gave a roar and struggled to his feet, pushing the remnants of the tent out of his way. He joined his staff to the queen's; their combined efforts slowly brought the group gently to the floor.

The fairies came around gradually and tried to flutter feebly to their feet; the shockwave seemed to have rendered their wings useless. Foxes, deer and stoats tried to stand on wobbly legs. Gwenyn flew over to her bees and buzzed at them encouragingly as they came to their senses.

Queen Rhosyn searched the boiling skies with a scowl. "Nesrin!" she screamed. "Show yourself!"

A high-pitched laugh echoed around the ravine, bouncing off the cliffs as thunder boomed in its wake. Lightning flashed, illuminating a figure standing on a high precipice, surrounded by nocturnal creatures; bats, owls and giant moths flapped around it, creating the illusion of monstrous wings. An army of dark creatures stepped up to join them.

Queen Rhosyn focused on the dark figure and zapped a glowing rainbow at it; the arc burst through the winged creatures, dispersing them as they shrieked and dived. Archers took aim as they came within range, picking the leaders off easily. The rest wheeled off and swooped hard and low, claws raking at the unicorns, who reared and shook their heads in their efforts to fight them off.

With a shout, Otto surged forward and extended

his shield over the terrified unicorns. The golden canopy blinded the bats, who shrieked and flew back up the cliff face, where Nesrin watched in fury.

"Attack them, you fools!" she screamed at the diminished bats, who turned and aimed for Gwenyn. The queen bee buzzed angrily as the horde of bats arrowed for her bees, snapping at them in the air and shaking them furiously in their cruel mouths.

Felicity shot swift and true, watching with satisfaction as bats fell down the ravine. The cloud of bees swarmed the remainder and sliced at them with their vicious stingers. Gwenyn buzzed in victory, watching the remaining bats fly off back into the forest. Nesrin screamed after them in rage.

Octavia and Martha took advantage of the lull in attack to race under the canopy, joining Otto in calming the unicorns. Soren, badly bleeding from a duel with a gigantic eagle owl, crawled under the canopy, breathing heavily.

"Open my bag," he said, wincing as he thrust the bag at Octavia. "There are sap bandages inside."

She did as he asked and found a roll of sticky brown leaf bandages, which she handed to him.

Struggling, he tried to unroll the bandages one-handed. Martha knelt to help as Mum joined them.

"Here," she said, wrapping a bandage around the gash across his arm. "I have had my fair share of injuries to bandage– my husband is clumsy with the pruning knife!" She smiled wistfully.

"Thank you," Soren murmured gratefully. The colour started to return to his cheeks as the sap did its magic and stemmed the flow.

"Soren!" Evony shouted frantically as she dived under the canopy as well. "Are you hurt?" She raked her eyes over him, looking for injuries.

Octavia and Martha exchanged a small grin at Evony's sudden worry over Soren, who slumped against a rock weakly as he gathered his strength.

"I think he'll be fine," Mum reassured Evony gently.

A screech in the distance had the princess turning, her eyes widening at the flames encircling the camp. Dark figures rushed up, shooting fire at logs and tree stumps.

"Fire imps," Evony said in horror. A white shape leaped over her, long ears spinning, creating a flurry of snow that blanketed pockets of fire. "Eira, I'm coming!" Evony yelled, and leapt into action after her mother's hare.

"Evony!" Soren shouted at her retreating form. "I have to help her!" He made to get up, but Mum held him back.

"You are too weak! The best thing you can do is help Otto move the unicorns into the waterfall pool; the flames won't get them there," she reasoned.

He looked at the place where Evony had disappeared, but nodded and allowed Mum to help him up. He and Otto led the unicorns back into the pool, the protective

canopy shielding them.

Martha, still holding the roll of bandages, looked around at the wounded fairies and creatures. "I'm going to help the injured," she told the others.

"Be safe," Octavia said, and followed Mum over to where Felicity stood, scanning the skies.

"Nesrin has disappeared," she told them. "The queen and king followed her to that ledge. I fear it's a trap."

A volley of arrows shot from above the ledge and had them running for cover behind a large group of rocks; Octavia's foot connected with something small and furry. She looked down and was greeted with the cowering form of Wattle.

"You! You little weasel!" She grabbed him by the scruff of his neck. "You betrayed us!" She shook him roughly.

"Please don't hurt me! My queen is still angry with me, so I am hiding until this is all over," he whimpered, eyes rolling in his head.

"Octavia, put him down. Maybe he can tell us where Beatrice is," Mum said softly, crouching to Wattle's level.

"Oh yes, kind Key Keeper, kind human lady," he simpered, patting her dusty leggings.

The smoke had nearly reached them, and Octavia could hear the frightened whinnies and neighs of the terrified unicorns. Eira bounded by in a blur of white, shooting a stream of glittering flakes in their direction and blanketing the ground with cool, powdery snow.

"She is at Castle Astra, but there are only a handful of guards there. Queen Nesrin wanted to hit you with the full force of her army," Wattle said, a little too proudly, making Mum narrow her violet-blue eyes at him.

A buzzing sounded in Octavia's ear, and she saw Gwenyn hovering by her side. "It izzz not zafe here! My beezzz will lift you out, before the zmoke reachezzz them and overcomezzz uzzz all," she told them.

Wattle took advantage of their distraction and scampered away into the smoke. Octavia made to go after him, but the carpet of bees landed at their feet and she was urged to get on by her mother.

Mum, Felicity and Octavia crouched low on the bees as they rose higher and higher, out of reach of the incoming, intoxicating smoke. The bees settled onto the top of the cliff, where Aurus could be seen locking horns with a black stag with orange eyes. They were safe from the fire, but danger still awaited all around them.

"Please, Queen Gwenyn, can your bees find Martha?" Octavia pleaded. "She was helping the injured."

Gwenyn peered down and saw that the smoke was clearing. Her buzz had her swarm lifting and diving once again into the battle below.

A roll of thunder echoed around the ravine as Taran swooped into sight, followed by Nesrin's cloud. She stepped from it and gave a sardonic smile.

"I said you would not win," she told Octavia as Taran circled overhead, booming loudly.

Octavia smiled, to Nesrin's evident confusion, for behind Nesrin stood Queen Rhosyn, King Llyffant and an army of speckled toads. King Llyffant caught Octavia's eyes and winked as the amphibious creatures hopped forward and wrapped their long tongues around Nesrin's arms, knocking her staff from her hand.

With a scream of rage, Nesrin looked down and shuddered in horror. Queen Rhosyn and King Llyffant aimed their staffs above Nesrin, two rainbows arcing from their tips, joining in a sparkle of light. The light beams solidified into a shining golden cage, which dropped silently over Nesrin as the toads retracted their tongues.

Nesrin turned on her sister. "How dare you!" She tried to grab the shining bars of her cage but yelped as if they had burned her.

"How dare *you?*" Queen Rhosyn shot back, fury written across her beautiful face. "You curse the last true believers, thus endangering the whole of our realm! You decimate the Flower Fields! Kidnap one of our guests! Wage war upon us!" She paced in front of her sister, sparks flying from her in her anger.

"Well, why wouldn't I? You have it all! *You* get to rule the realm," Nesrin shrieked. "Along with your toady husband," she added with a sneer in the direction of King Llyffant, who bowed sarcastically.

The battle on the clifftop had stopped as Nesrin's guard realised she had been captured; they slunk away into the shadows, watchful and waiting. Aurus, one magnificent antler broken, limped over to stand next to his queen. His eyes were locked upon Nesrin, who gave a sudden smile.

"But you do not have the one thing I do – I have been harnessing the power from Prince Kiran's descendant. I saw it lying dormant within her, but I have been feeding it. She grows stronger by the hour. Her silly grandmother thwarted my attempt at rule all those years ago, but I have another chance; look!" she commanded.

A beam of light shot from the top of Castle Astra, lightning zigzagging across the sky.

Nesrin laughed. "Soon her power will reach Castle Enfys and lay it to ruin, and I will rule while you all stand in the dust!"

Queen Rhosyn exchanged a worried look with King Llyffant; murmurs came from the assembled crowd as more of the guard joined them. Nesrin gazed avidly at her castle, waiting for the next beam of light.

The carpet of bees landed next to Octavia and upon it sat Otto and Martha, tunics torn and dusty.

"The fire is out," Otto announced. "Eira and the water fairies drove the fire imps back. Soren is looking after the unicorns, and the healing fairies are seeing to the injured. Evony is headed up here." He put his foot out to step down, but Octavia shook her head; grabbing Felicity, she headed over to Gwenyn.

"Can you take us to Castle Astra? Beatrice will *have* to listen to us now we have Otto," she whispered to the queen bee. "Hopefully she'll realise we can all go back home, and life can get back to normal. We have to act now!"

Gwenyn buzzed worriedly as she decided what to do. A gasp from the crowd forced her decision, as a larger beam of light shot from the distant castle.

"I will take you," she buzzed. Octavia made sure Ferren was still secure in her pocket and stepped with Felicity onto the bee platform. They settled themselves next to Otto and Martha and nodded at Gwenyn, who rose slowly.

Mum, distracted by the light, didn't see them going until the last minute. "Octavia!" she shouted exasperatedly at the retreating swarm, but it was too late.

Fifteen

From the Dust

GWENYN URGED HER BEES ON TO CASTLE ASTRA. Under cover of the dark clouds, they were able to get close before they were spotted. Felicity took aim and released an arrow, hitting a guard whose eyes had widened at the sight of the incoming cloud of bees, the magical arrow knocking him out.

They swooped into the roofless throne room. Beatrice stood in the centre, an invisible wind swirling her gown around her ankles and whipping her loose hair across her marble-white face.

With two rapid arrow shots, Felicity made short work of the guards who charged into the room, beating their black wings furiously. Otto watched his older sister, admiration shining in his gleaming violet-blue eyes. The

bees hovered as Octavia and the others stepped from them.

Beatrice looked at them with wild eyes. "Stay back!" she shrieked. "I can't stop it!" She ended on a sob as another burst of light travelled from her chest, along her arm and shot through the staff she clutched.

"Bea, remember who you are and what we came here for," Martha pleaded, taking tentative steps toward her twin. "Look! Otto is safe. Tavi got the cure from Mum and Dad and Uncle Kit – they are waiting for you back home. We can all go back home together." she held out her hands beseechingly, tears welling in her blue eyes.

Beatrice shuddered, her hand convulsing on the staff. Her eyes travelled to Otto, who was standing next to Octavia, widening in disbelief. She clutched her head in pain and dropped to her knees as another burst of light racked her slim frame.

"We have to do something!" Octavia said frantically.

Martha rushed forward as if she couldn't stand to see her twin in pain any longer. She cradled Beatrice in her arms and held tight; despite the glow building within her sister, she didn't let her go. Beatrice writhed and twisted in Martha's embrace, pain etched across her face.

Octavia, seeing what Martha was trying to do, grabbed Otto and Felicity and ran forward. They encircled the pair and hung on, linked as one.

Octavia closed her eyes. The tingling in her fingers she had experienced before came back with a vengeance,

and focusing on that, she put all her love and faith into the forefront of her mind and believed. Believed with all her heart in her family. Believed that they would all be going back home safe together.

She opened her eyes and gasped; the glow within Beatrice was building until it was almost blinding. Octavia struggled to hold on, but feeling Felicity's and Otto's hands in hers and Ferren nestled in her pocket over her heart gave her strength. With one final thought of her family, she *believed!*

The glow in Beatrice pulsed once… twice… before fluttering out.

Beatrice sagged to the floor. The staff dropped from her hand onto the unforgiving stone, where it shattered in two. The silver orb rolled from the tip and lay empty and useless. Octavia, Otto, Felicity and Martha looked at each other in the aftermath, breathing heavily.

"Martha, whatever happened to your clothes?" a small voice whispered from the floor.

With a strangled sob, Martha looked at her softly smiling sister. "Bea!" she cried, helping her sister sit up and grabbing her in a tight hug that, this time, was reciprocated.

The grins exchanged by Otto, Octavia and Felicity were quickly extinguished as the floor beneath their feet began to tremble. The walls started to crumble and black rocks fell all around them.

"The Caztle'zzz defenze zyztem hazzz been turned

on! Nezrin'zzz magic izzz zuch that she hazzz zpelled Castle Aztra to fall, should it be taken," Gwenyn buzzed frantically.

The five reunited Blooms hastily climbed back onto the rapidly buzzing bees, clutching at each other as the bees lifted abruptly. All around them the castle was falling, lights flickering out one by one as they were showered in clouds of dust. The bees soared through the open roof as the castle toppled in on itself. Octavia looked down in horror at the castle ruins as a long, keening wail echoed across the sky, followed by one solitary clap of thunder.

The bees flew back to the clifftop and set the cousins down gently where Mum waited. She stood, legs planted, hands on her hips and eyes fierce, although they softened as Beatrice stumbled toward her.

"Beatrice!" she cried, running to hold her close. She ran her hands over her niece's hair and smiled into her eyes. "I am so happy to see you."

"And I you, Aunt Genny." Beatrice smiled back. She gently withdrew from the embrace to approach the queen, and curtsied tremulously. "I am so sorry for all the trouble I have caused," she said quietly.

Queen Rhosyn smiled benevolently at her. "My child, it was not your doing: you were bewitched by my own jealous sister." She looked sadly at Nesrin, who was on her knees in her cage, head bowed in defeat.

In a sudden move, Nesrin leapt to her feet. "I will not be thwarted! You may have destroyed my castle, but I

will take yours!" she screeched, her face contorted into a furious mask of hatred. "Taran!" she yelled at her circling raven.

Before anyone could stop him, Taran swooped low and scooped up Nesrin's fallen staff. He spiralled back into the clouds and swirled faster and faster, whipping the clouds into a boiling tempest, funnelling it toward the cage. With a crack, the cage shattered and Nesrin stood triumphant, her hand outstretched to catch her staff as Taran flew toward her.

With a gigantic leap into the sky, using his large wings to propel himself up, King Llyffant intercepted the raven and knocked the staff from his beak. It clattered over the clifftop and came to rest at Beatrice's feet.

Nesrin laughed confidently. "Girl, give it to me," she said, her tone coaxing.

Beatrice paused and looked at the staff at her feet. Octavia felt her heart begin to pound in her chest as she watched Nesrin's triumphant grin creep across her cruel face. Beatrice slowly raised her gaze and looked at Nesrin for a long moment, before turning to meet the identical eyes of her sister.

A huge smile lit Beatrice's face. She bent to grasp the staff with one hand and placed the other on top of it, palm down. Martha beamed and placed hers on top.

"What are you doing?" Nesrin screeched, uncertainty colouring her voice.

Felicity grinned and placed her hand next, swiftly

followed by Octavia, who nodded at Otto. As his hand completed the bond, a light glowed from their combined hands. The children gasped as it rushed through them and into the staff, shattering it into a thousand fragments.

"Nooooo!" screamed Nesrin. "What magic is this?" Enraged, she turned to Queen Rhosyn, who held her own staff at her sister.

"That, sister dear, is the most powerful magic of all – one you will never tap into." Queen Rhosyn grasped the hands of her husband and daughter, who walked to her mother's side; their combined power flowed through them, creating an aura that lit up the dark skies.

Nesrin seemed to diminish before them, her wings drooping and her head bowed in defeat. Octavia was just wondering what Nesrin would do next when the dark fairy reached into her robes and drew out a vial. Before she could be stopped, she uncorked it and drank deeply.

"Nessy, stop!" Queen Rhosyn cried, but her sister could not be helped – in fact, she was her sister no more, and in her place flapped another black raven with wings of silver feathers. It circled the group once, gave a loud caw, and shot up to join Taran. With a boom, the two ravens flew off. Queen Rhosyn watched until they were two specks in the lightening sky.

With a sigh, she turned to the Blooms. "You are safe now."

Mum let out a breath and looked at Octavia. "Not quite yet," she admonished. "You and I need to have a

little chat about your tendency to run off headfirst into danger."

Everybody laughed as Octavia gulped audibly and Ferren gave a frightened squeak, crawling back into the safety of Octavia's pocket, while Pan tweeted disapprovingly overhead.

The wounded had been tended to and were resting, and the able had been dispatched to capture the last of Nesrin's guard still lurking nearby.

Octavia and Otto sat side by side, watching the sun rise together, the light playing over their copper curls. Martha and Felicity sat nearby and filled Beatrice in about what had happened in her absence; in turn, Beatrice told them that she had no real memory of her time with Nesrin – just flashes here and there.

"But what I don't understand is how I was able to perform magic."

"I can answer that for you." With Eira bounding at her heels, Queen Rhosyn glided over, her gown luminous in the sunrise, the rays picking out the purples, greens and blues. "We have a common ancestor in Prince Kiran's family – he married a mortal girl, and the Blooms are descended from one of their daughters. Nesrin and I are descended from Prince Kiran's sister, who became queen following his abdication. You, Beatrice, it seems, have an extraordinary amount of his magical blood running through your veins. My sister was always excellent at sensing power. She took advantage of your magical lineage, using you as a conduit to enhance her power. You all have some magical blood, but it has been diluted so much over the years that it is rare for a human to perform real fairy magic," she added musingly.

She stared thoughtfully at Octavia and Otto, the latter of which was giggling at Ferren's antics as Pan teased the mouse with a juicy red berry, flying just out of reach.

"Maybe it is time for a change," the queen murmured to herself. She nodded to the children as she gracefully rose and went to join her own family.

The journey back to Castle Enfys was a much more light-hearted affair; the unicorns pranced joyously, their coats a splendid bouquet of colour lighting up the track ahead.

"I cannot wait to see Mum and Dad," Beatrice announced as she rode happily upon Caeruleus, patting his neck affectionately. Octavia thought her cousin was practically glowing. Her long hair was now braided and intertwined with small blue flowers, and her dark dress had been changed for comfortable leggings and a tunic.

"Me too," Martha agreed, "although... I am actually

going to miss it here." She looked around Rhosyn's Woods, where various woodland creatures observed them as they passed. In doing so, she missed the startled looks her words caused in the other children.

With a laugh, Octavia urged Xanthe forward to join Otto, who greeted her with a smile; they rode together through Bloomsville Village to where Finnian waited nervously. His eyes lit up when he saw Soren.

"Ah, my son, you are returned safely!" he said, his voice full of relief, flapping up to pat Soren on his broad back.

"Well met, father," Soren replied, vaulting from Ember smoothly, the sap bandages having worked their magic and healed his wounds. He helped round up all the unicorns to take them back to the paddock.

Xanthe looked deep into Octavia's eyes.

"I will miss you," Octavia told her as she ran her hand along her soft nose. Xanthe gave a whinny and shook her head. To her delight, Octavia saw a flower materialise from Xanthe's horn and float into Octavia's outstretched hand. The yellow flower tinkled as if it was made of crystal. "Thank you!" Octavia said with tears in her eyes.

She watched as Xanthe walked over to join the herd, a ball of sadness sitting in the pit of her stomach and the tears threatening to fall.

Mum came up behind her and gently hugged her. "Time to go home," she murmured.

With one last look at the unicorns and a final wave

to Soren, who had been talking closely with Evony, the Blooms headed up the winding path to the castle.

They entered the castle gates to great fanfare; the Fairy Court was all assembled to welcome them back. Octavia smiled happily at Briar, Sorrel, Alora, Haf and Hevva as they waved at her from amongst the crowd.

Queen Rhosyn held up her staff, and quiet reigned instantly. "I would like everyone to please join us in the grand hall for a celebration banquet," she announced.

The assembled group cheered and headed for the grand hall, where flowers still adorned every available surface and hung suspended from the ceiling in long trains, remnants of the Late Summer Ball. Food and drink was served with the flick of a wand from the food fairies, Cegin proudly orchestrating it all.

"Please, a toast to our human friends, for friends they have become." Queen Rhosyn looked down the table at the children, took a deep breath, exchanged a look with the king – who nodded encouragingly back – and continued, "During the conflict with my sister, things were different and restricted in Fairy Land. but I feel we are long overdue for a change. It is time I took the power back into my hands. Therefore, I hereby decree that the Blooms will always be welcome in Fairy Land, and would indeed encourage them to visit us here to strengthen our bond, for after all we could not exist without their belief in us." The queen raised her elderflower wine and toasted them: "To the Blooms!" It was echoed throughout the court.

Octavia exchanged excited looks with her siblings and cousins. They could come back! Mum caught Octavia's grin and groaned good-naturedly.

Octavia's attention was brought back to Queen Rhosyn, who was speaking to her. "Are you ready to go home, Octavia Bloom?"

Octavia glanced around at her fairy friends and back at her family, violet-blue eyes shining brightly with the knowledge that she could always come back.

"Yes. It's time."

"It was a pleasure meeting you, young Key Keeper," King Llyffant said in his deep voice, bowing low over Octavia's hand. "I have you to thank for being reunited with my queen."

Octavia smiled happily back and turned to Evony, who was hugging Felicity. "I will look after your bow and arrow until you return," Evony said, and Felicity reluctantly relinquished her precious bow.

"Thank you for helping me prove myself to my

mother," Evony directed at Octavia with a wink. Octavia winked back and gave her a swift hug. Leaving Evony to say goodbye to the others, she looked sadly at Ferren.

"I will miss you the most," she told her.

"It is not for long." Ferren patted her face with her tiny paws. "You will be ten soon, and at your Key Keeper ceremony I will be able to come and live with you." Octavia stroked her gently and joined Otto as he took his leave of the queen.

"Thank you for looking after my son," Mum told Queen Rhosyn, who beamed at Otto's joyful face.

"It has been our pleasure," Queen Rhosyn replied as the king, Evony and Eira came to join her. Taking her staff, she activated the Portal.

Octavia swiftly passed Ferren to Evony, before gripping hands with Otto as the rest of her family followed suit. She stared at the Portal in awe as the rainbow crystals started to glow. As one, they all stepped into the shimmering opening; Queen Rhosyn met Octavia's eyes. She smiled.

"Goodbye for now."

Octavia nodded and closed her eyes. When she opened them again, they were all back in the attic at Castle Bloom.

Sixteen

The Key Keepers

"Bea? Matty?" a trembling voice asked. "Am I dreaming?"

Aunt Anastasia hesitantly walked forward into the patch of dappled sunlight, a thin blanket wrapped around her trembling shoulders.

"Mum!" Beatrice cried out, then, with a sob, ran forward and was caught in her mother's safe embrace. Martha joined them, clinging tightly, tears running down her face. The three slid to the floor, crying and laughing at the same time.

"Genny," a soft voice called from the doorway.

Mum turned to see Dad standing there, his face pale and his hair sticking up in tufts. With a cry, she ran forward and hugged him tightly. Over her shoulder, Dad's

eyes roved across his children's faces, stopping on Otto's, where they widened.

"Otto?" Dad said, his breath hitching. He slowly untangled himself from Mum and walked toward his son. Mum looked on with misty eyes as Pan settled on her shoulder.

Octavia grinned impishly as she watched her father solemnly offer his hand to Otto, who in turn threw himself into Dad's arms.

"Dad," he said happily as a cloud of fur barrelled through the doorway, narrowly missing knocking Mum off her feet. Otto found himself licked exuberantly as Bronwen pushed her way in between them, and just like that, Otto was finally home.

"I thought I would find you here!" An amused voice startled Octavia out of her daydream.

Sitting on the window seat in the attic, she had been staring at the skirting board where the Fairy Door always appeared. Bronwen had taken to following her about like a shadow, and was watching her warily out of one eye as she lay curled up in the patch of sunlight on the floor.

"You're going to miss the ceremony – and we can't have a Key Keeper ceremony without the Key Keeper," Felicity said, coming over to stand next to her sister,

patting the dog as she passed. Bronwen's tail wagged lazily. "Come on," she added, grasping Octavia's hand and pulling her up.

Octavia gasped as the beam of light shot from their hands and revealed the Fairy Door again.

"Don't even think about it!" Felicity warned as Octavia threw a mischievous look over her shoulder. Bronwen sat up with a bark of agreement.

"Look! There's another note and a bottle of fairy dust!" Octavia exclaimed, clutching her sister in excitement. She bent to retrieve them, savouring the scent of mossy ground. The note was warm as if it had been sitting in the summer sun, whilst the bottle of dust tingled in her fingers.

"Come on, let's go and show the others!" Octavia rushed from the attic. Felicity laughed and followed behind her, trying to keep up. Bronwen skidded on the flagstones in her own haste to catch up.

Octavia dashed into the ballroom, where preparations were under way for the Key Keeper ceremony.

"Ah, there she is." Mum came over to hug her youngest daughter. "Are you ready?"

"Yes, I can't wait – but, Mum, look at this!" She thrust the bottle and note into her mother's already full hands. Laughing, Mum hastily put down the box of flower garlands and looked incredulously at the tiny bottle and note.

Everyone else crowded around curiously.

"Where did this come from?" Dad asked suspiciously, narrowing his eyes at Octavia.

She held up her hands. "The door appeared again when Fliss helped me up – they were outside it," she explained earnestly.

"Well, open it, then," Great-Aunt Clara said, looking at the tiny note as Grandmother eyed Octavia with an indulgent smile.

"'Throw the dust into a sunbeam'," Mum read aloud, looking quizzically at the others.

"Here, Mum." Otto pulled her over to the large window that dominated the room. Sunlight streamed through it, a large beam spotlighting the floor.

Mum looked at Aunt Anastasia, who shrugged and nodded, so Mum un-stoppered the bottle, peeling away the gold wax seal. She hesitated, before throwing the dust into the sunbeam, where it glittered and flickered like an old TV set. Finally, the flickering stopped, and an image came into view; it was Queen Rhosyn, resplendent in a shimmering golden gown, her wings extended majestically. She looked around before her gaze landed on the assembled Blooms.

The Blooms curtsied and bowed hastily as the queen bestowed a glittering smile upon them. "Blessings to you all on this most special day. We in Fairy Land will be celebrating and toasting to the new Key Keepers." She looked at Octavia, whose mouth opened in surprise.

"Key Keepers? As in more than one?" she blurted,

perplexed.

Queen Rhosyn nodded and looked at Otto. "Young Bloom son, throughout the generations there has never been a boy child born with copper curls and violet-blue eyes, which therefore makes you special indeed. The king and I have agreed that you *and* Octavia will become joint Key Keepers."

Octavia gasped and clutched Otto in excitement. Queen Rhosyn continued, smiling indulgently at the pair.

"The male of your line will now be included in keeping the secret of the Fairy Door safe." She looked at Mum, who was clutching Dad's hand tightly. "The men in your family have proven they are loyal friends of Fairy Land – and besides, it was an archaic rule," Queen Rhosyn added, "one I can and shall change."

"Does that mean I get a companion too?" Otto asked, his boyish voice ending on a squeak of excitement.

The queen nodded. "We have someone very special waiting to join you. Blessings on you all, and I hope to see you in Fairy Land soon," she added, including Martha and Beatrice in her look.

The image faded away, leaving glitter sparkling in the air.

"Well," Grandmother breathed out. "I need a cup of tea," she announced, and left the room to find Mrs Fawcett.

"Me too," Great-Aunt Clara said. "Come, Rowan." The squirrel had been gazing at the spot where the queen

had stood, but scampered over to leave the room with Great-Aunt Clara.

Otto and Octavia were dancing around the room; they circled over to Felicity, Martha and Beatrice and linked arms with them. Laughingly, they all joined in, joy shining from their happy faces as Mum, Dad, Aunt Anastasia and Uncle Piers looked on.

"Come on, let's finish getting this ceremony set up," Mum told them eventually, clapping her hands. The five children stopped dancing and picked up boxes of garlands and bows, helping to finish decorating the hall. Pan was being especially helpful by flying to the hard-to-reach corners and attaching the flowering garlands.

Finally satisfied, Mum addressed her twins. "All right, you two – time to get changed. Mrs Fawcett has laid out your clothes in your rooms. And you too, girls; your clothes are in Martha and Beatrice's room, Felicity."

Otto and Octavia left the ballroom and galloped up to their rooms, the others following more sedately. Octavia gasped in delight as she saw the beautiful yellow dress draped on her bed. She picked it up, admiring how it shimmered in the light. Creeping vines and yellow buds had been delicately embroidered along the hem, and tiny rainbow-coloured crystals were scattered across the bodice.

She put it on and admired herself in the mirror. As a final touch, she tucked the yellow crystal flower, presented to her by Xanthe nearly two months ago now, into her

already braided crown of flaming hair.

Octavia could hear the voices of her sister and cousins as they made their way back down the corridor. Giving them a minute to reach the ballroom, she slowly walked out into the corridor, feeling subdued by the importance of what was about to be bestowed upon her. She was met by a solemn Otto, looking the part in a copper-coloured waistcoat embroidered with orange flowers and rainbow crystals winking along the hem.

The pair clutched hands and walked quietly down the stairs, Octavia's yellow satin shoes making no noise on the faded carpet.

Rainbow candles in heavy silver candelabras lined the walkway into the ballroom, flickering as the pair passed them. Mum, beaming with pride and radiant in a flowing, multicoloured dress, met them at the door and led them into the room. Various Bloom relations had come to join in the celebrations. Cascades of flowers spilled from huge urns on either side of a raised platform.

Octavia and Otto took their places opposite their mother on the platform. Felicity, Beatrice, and Martha smiled widely at them, dressed in beautiful, shimmering dresses of their own.

Grandmother, as the current custodian of Castle Bloom, stood at the front of the platform in a splendid pewter dress, her charm bracelet jingling from her slim wrist, the setting sun a halo around her head.

"Thank you to you all for attending tonight. We are

here to bestow upon Octavia and Otto the esteemed title of Key Keeper," Grandmother began, her voice echoing off the stone walls. "In my objective of keeping our family safe, I hid the key for many years..." She paused. "...But now, the key couldn't be in safer hands," she finished, beaming at her youngest grandchildren.

"To Octavia and Otto, Key Keepers!" she announced as Mum held out the tiny glowing key.

Light rippled from Mum's hand over to Octavia's and Otto's. The intermittent tingling Octavia had been experiencing buzzed up her arm like an electric shock as a feeling of warmth filled her whole body. Looking at Otto, she could see a dazed look on his face.

"Wow!" he said, and took a long breath.

Octavia took the key reverently and placed the vine necklace over Otto's head. "You look after it for now," she told him, to rapturous applause and cheers from the assembled Blooms. Bronwen, a satin bow tied around her shaggy neck, barked twice.

Pan and Rowan suddenly hurried from the ballroom, and Mum and Great-Aunt Clara turned to look at one another knowingly. Within minutes the creatures were back, but they were not alone.

"Ferren!" Octavia shouted, jumping off the platform, her shoes sliding on the smooth stone floor. She knelt and caught Ferren as she scampered into her hands and up to her shoulder, giggling as the mouse tickled her cheek with her tiny whiskers.

A handsome brown otter stood on the threshold of the ballroom, sniffing the air, his whiskers twitching. His eyes locked with Otto, who hesitantly walked toward him. He knelt next to the otter and smiled as he twitched his nose, looking at Otto with his clever eyes.

Otto nodded and announced to the crowd, "His name is Sage, and he is my new companion."

Everyone clapped and crowded around to welcome Ferren and Sage to Castle Bloom.

"I'll expect you two to look after our two adventurers!" Dad shouted to the creatures above the din, to which everyone laughed.

The celebrations lasted well into the night. Octavia's mind was aswirl with new faces and names; she hadn't known there were so many Blooms she had never met before.

After the last of the guests had retired to the guest tower for the night, Octavia took Ferren on a tour of the castle. Finally, they made their way to the drawing room, where her immediate family were assembled, drinking a last cup of tea before bed.

Octavia grinned as she caught Grandmother breaking off a piece of shortbread and absentmindedly feeding it to Rowan. He raised a bushy eyebrow at a chuckling Great-Aunt Clara. Patting her sister with renewed affection, Great-Aunt Clara heaved herself up to pour more tea.

Mum beckoned Octavia over as she hugged a sleepy Otto against her. Sage lay curled on his lap.

"I think it's time we had a little talk about your habit of running headfirst into danger."

Octavia looked up as Dad spoke quietly, but her father was not looking at her; he was looking at Mum with an amused twinkle in his eye.

Mum raised guilty violet-blue eyes to Octavia's matching ones, and the pair burst out laughing.

The laughter was almost magical as it rippled around the room, echoing through the castle and up into the attic, where a tiny door was waiting to be revealed once more.

In the ruins of Castle Astra, something was stirring. Dusty black and silver feathers ruffled in the darkness, the raven they belonged to trying to get comfortable. Anger, a bright shining spear, was not enough to keep her warm, but the thirst for vengeance kept her alive.

Her time would come; oh yes, she would rise from the dust and take back what had been stolen from her.

She opened one silver eye and focused it far into the distance, where a shining white castle stood tall and proud, in its depths a hidden Portal to the world of humans.

Glossary of Names

Octavia	(Oc-tay-vee-ah)	Chosen because she was born in October
Tavi	(Tay-vee)	Nickname
Felicity	(Fuh-liss-i-tee)	Latin meaning Happiness
Martha	(Mar-thuh)	Aramaic meaning Lady
Beatrice	(Bee-ah-triss)	Latin meaning Blessed
Evelyn	(Eh-veh-lyn)	English meaning Life
Bronwen	(Bron-wen)	Welsh meaning White
Clara	(Clar-ah)	Latin meaning Bright / Clear
Rowan	(Roe-wan)	Little Red-haired one
Mrs Fawcett	(Mrs-Four-set)	
Genevieve	(Jen-eh-veeve)	French meaning Woman of the Family
Anastasia	(Ann-ah-stay-zee-ah)	Greek meaning Resurrection
Pan	(Pann)	God of flocks
Otto	(Ot-toe)	German meaning Prosperity
Arianthe	Ah-ree-ann-thee	Purple Flower
Ferren	Feh-renn	Derived from Ferrous/Iron Grey
Lyffy	Lih-ffee	Nickname
Feargal	Fee-ar-gal	Irish meaning Brave
Evony	Ev-uh-nee	French meaning archer
Rhosyn	Roe-zin	Little Rose
Eira	Ay-ruh	Welsh meaning Snow
Enfys	En-vis	Welsh meaning Rainbow
Nesrin	Nez-rin	Wild Rose
Taran	Tah-ran	Welsh meaning Thunder
Alora	Ah-lor-ah	Light

Briar	Bry-ah	Prickly shrub
Sorrel	Soh-rrel	Plant with arrow-shaped leaves
Hevva	Heh-va	Cornish
Aloysius	Al-oh-ish-ush	French meaning Warrior
Aurus	Awe-rus	Latin meaning Golden
Haf	Hav	Welsh meaning Summer
Wyvern	Why-vern	2-legged dragon
Finnian	Fin-ee-ann	Gaelic meaning White / Fair
Xanthe	Zan-thee	Greek for Golden / Yellow
Linnea	Lin-ee-uh	Small Pink Flower
Emeraude	Em-er-owed	French meaning Emerald
Caeruleus	kiy-ru-lee-us	Latin meaning Dark Blue
Ione	I-own-ee	Greek meaning Violet
Soren	Soh-ren	Danish meaning Stern
Ember	Em-burr	Smouldering pieces
Wattle	What-ull	Australian Acacia plant
Gwenyn	Gwen-in	Welsh meaning Bee
Astra	As-trah	Latin for Star
Llyffant	Liff-ant	Welsh meaning Toad
Kit	Kit	Short for Christopher meaning to Bear / Carry
Piers	Pears	Old English meaning Rock
Cegin	Keh-gin	Welsh meaning Kitchen
Oren	O-ren	Welsh meaning Orange
Fides	Fiy-ds	Latin meaning Faithful
Sage	Sayge	Wise

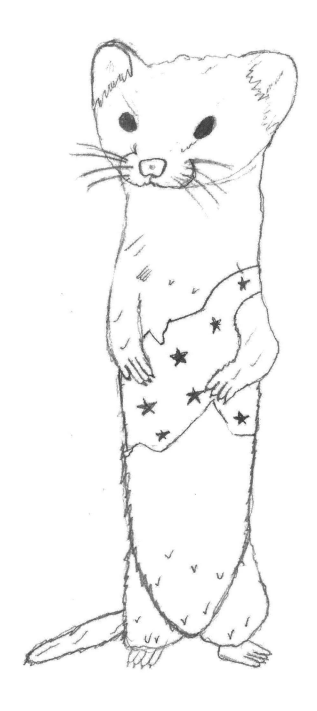

Acknowledgements

Every heroine needs a great team beside them to complete their quest. This journey was no different. Heartfelt thanks to...

My amazing editor Emma, who with her magic eyes and quill helped me to see how much more wondrous this tale could be.

My fabulous readers: Anna and Sarah Jane for their honest and helpful feedback. You shaped this story with your insightful thoughts and suggestions, and to my niece Shannon who enjoyed it so much, she read it in one night.

My magical twin and fellow author Madonna for your never-ending support and fairy inspiration – watch out for those glitter sneezes!

The super-supportive writing community, who motivated me daily and encouraged me when the quest seemed hopeless.

My fairy godmother Caroline and her 'magic one' Hayley Ann for being the first to set eyes on this book and for introducing me to the enchanting world of Fairy Doors.

My mother Heather who instilled her love of books and reading into my heart from a young age, (and for believing me when I was convinced fairies lived at the bottom of our garden.)

Our crazy dog Patch, who was my own Fairy Companion and the inspiration for one of my favourite characters, (Can you guess which one? I'll give you a clue – he eats too much and likes to steal things!)

My amazing children who inspire me every day: Adam; your wondrous art skills helped me to envision my characters, bringing them to life. Chloe, my brain-storming buddy and fellow fairy-lover; thank you for listening to the story and enjoying it as much as I enjoyed writing it. Nathan, my mini author-in-the-making; thank you for believing in me and being proud of my writing. Jake; thank you for your comic relief on the hard days and for your amazing squishy hugs.

And finally, my wonderful husband Dean; thank you for making my dreams come true. Love is truly the most powerful magic of all.

Coming November 2020…

Beatrice Bloom
and the
Star Crystal

Beatrice Bloom is excited but a bit apprehensive to be heading through the fairy door once again with her sister and cousins.

The adventure quickly turns ominous with the arrival of old foes and new enemies who are conspiring to overthrow the throne.

Is Beatrice brave enough to embrace magic once more to help her friends? And can she restore the star crystal to its rightful place before time runs out?

Beatrice will need all her courage in this new 'Through the Fairy Door' Adventure.

Courage, friendship and deceit collide in this spellbinding adventure.

About the Author

When not searching the backs of wardrobes for Narnia or exploring yet another Castle, Estelle can be found with her nose in a book or a pen in her hand.

Having previously worked at Cardiff Castle, she now writes full time while looking after her four children.

She lives on the beautiful South Wales coast with her husband, children and crazy dog.

This is her debut novel, the first in a series of five. She loves to connect with her readers and can be contacted on estellegracetudor.com or via her Instagram page @through_the_fairy_door_books

Printed in Great Britain
by Amazon